A REBELLIOUS HEROINE

John Kendrick Bangs

1st WORLD
LIBRARY
Literary Society

A Rebellious Heroine

J. K. Bangs

© 1st World Library – Literary Society, 2004
PO Box 2211
Fairfield, IA 52556
www.1stworldlibrary.org
First Edition

LCCN: 2005901338

Softcover ISBN: 1-4218-1153-7
Hardcover ISBN: 1-4218-1053-0
eBook ISBN: 1-4218-1253-3

Purchase *"A Rebellious Heroine"*
as a traditional bound book at:
www.1stWorldLibrary.org/purchase.asp?ISBN=1-4218-1153-7

1st World Library Literary Society is a nonprofit
organization dedicated to promoting literacy by:

- Creating a free internet library accessible from any
  computer worldwide.
- Hosting writing competitions and offering book
  publishing scholarships.

A Rebellious Heroine
contributed by Tim, Ed & Rodney
in support of
1st World Library Literary Society

CHAPTER I

STUART HARLEY: REALIST

"- if a word could save me, and that word were not the Truth, nay, if it did but swerve a hair's-breadth from the Truth, I would not say it!"

LONGFELLOW.

Stuart Harley, despite his authorship of many novels, still considered himself a realist. He affected to say that he did not write his books; that he merely transcribed them from life as he saw it, and he insisted always that he saw life as it was.

"The mission of the novelist, my dear Professor," he had once been heard to say at his club, "is not to amuse merely; his work is that of an historian, and he should be quite as careful to write truthfully as is the historian. How is the future to know what manner of lives we nineteenth century people have lived unless our novelists tell the truth?"

"Possibly the historians will tell them," observed the Professor of Mathematics. "Historians sometimes do tell us interesting things."

"True," said Harley. "Very true; but then what historian ever let you into the secret of the every-day life of the people of whom he writes? What historian ever so vitalized Louis the Fourteenth as Dumas has vitalized him? Truly, in reading mere history I have seemed to be reading of lay figures, not of men; but when the novelist has taken hold properly - ah, then we get the men."

"Then," objected the Professor, "the novelist is never to create a great character?"

"The humorist or the mere romancer may, but as for the novelist with a true ideal of his mission in life he would better leave creation to nature. It is blasphemy for a purely mortal being to pretend that he can create a more interesting character or set of characters than the Almighty has already provided for the use of himself and his brothers in literature; that he can involve these creations in a more dramatic series of events than it has occurred to an all-wise Providence to put into the lives of His creatures; that, by the exercise of that misleading faculty which the writer styles his imagination, he can portray phases of life which shall prove of more absorbing interest or of greater moral value to his readers than those to be met with in the every-day life of man as he is."

"Then," said the Professor, with a dexterous jab of his cue at the pool-balls - "then, in your estimation, an author is a thing to be led about by the nose by the beings he selects for use in his books?"

"You put it in a rather homely fashion," returned Harley; "but, on the whole, that is about the size of it."

"And all a man needs, then, to be an author is an eye and

a typewriting machine?" asked the Professor.

"And a regiment of detectives," drawled Dr. Kelly, the young surgeon, "to follow his characters about."

Harley sighed. Surely these men were unsympathetic.

"I can't expect you to grasp the idea exactly," he said, "and I can't explain it to you, because you'd become irreverent if I tried."

"No, we won't," said Kelly. "Go on and explain it to us - I'm bored, and want to be amused."

So Harley went on and tried to explain how the true realist must be an inspired sort of person, who can rise above purely physical limitations; whose eye shall be able to pierce the most impenetrable of veils; to whom nothing in the way of obtaining information as to the doings of such specimens of mankind as he has selected for his pages is an insurmountable obstacle.

"Your author, then, is to be a mixture of a New York newspaper reporter and the Recording Angel?" suggested Kelly.

"I told you you'd become irreverent," said Harley; "nevertheless, even in your irreverence, you have expressed the idea. The writer must be omniscient as far as the characters of his stories are concerned - he must have an eye which shall see all that they do, a mind sufficiently analytical to discern what their motives are, and the courage to put it all down truthfully, neither adding nor subtracting, coloring only where color is needed to make the moral lesson he is trying to teach stand out the more vividly."

"In short, you'd have him become a photographer," said the Professor.

"More truly a soulscape-painter," retorted Harley, with enthusiasm.

"Heavens!" cried the Doctor, dropping his cue with a loud clatter to the floor. "Soulscape! Here's a man talking about not creating, and then throws out an invention like soulscape! Harley, you ought to write a dictionary. With a word like soulscape to start with, it would sweep the earth!"

Harley laughed. He was a good-natured man, and he was strong enough in his convictions not to weaken for the mere reason that somebody else had ridiculed them. In fact, everybody else might have ridiculed them, and Harley would still have stood true, once he was convinced that he was right.

"You go on sawing people's legs off, Billy," he said, good-naturedly. "That's a thing you know about; and as for the Professor, he can go on showing you and the rest of mankind just why the shortest distance between two points is in a straight line. I'll take your collective and separate words for anything on the subject of surgery or mathematics, but when it comes to my work I wouldn't bank on your theories if they were endorsed by the Rothschilds."

"He'll never write a decent book in his life if he clings to that theory," said Kelly, after Harley had departed. "There's precious little in the way of the dramatic nowadays in the lives of people one cares to read about."

Nevertheless, Harley had written interesting books,

books which had brought him reputation, and what is termed genteel poverty - that is to say, his fame was great, considering his age, and his compensation was just large enough to make life painful to him. His income enabled him to live well enough to make a good appearance among, and share somewhat at their expense in the life of, others of far greater means; but it was too small to bring him many of the things which, while not absolutely necessities, could not well be termed luxuries, considering his tastes and his temperament. A little more was all he needed.

"If I could afford to write only when I feel like it," he said, "how happy I should be! But these orders - they make me a driver of men, and not their historian."

In fact, Harley was in that unfortunate, and at the same time happy, position where he had many orders for the product of his pen, and such financial necessities that he could not afford to decline one of them.

And it was this very situation which made his rebellious heroine of whom I have essayed to write so sore a trial to the struggling young author.

It was early in May, 1895, that Harley had received a note from Messrs. Herring, Beemer, & Chadwick, the publishers, asking for a story from his pen for their popular "Blue and Silver Series."

"The success of your Tiffin-Talk," they wrote, "has been such that we are prepared to offer you our highest terms for a short story of 30,000 words, or thereabouts, to be published in our 'Blue and Silver Series.' We should like to have it a love-story, if possible; but whatever it is, it must be characteristic, and ready for publication in

November. We shall need to have the manuscript by September 1st at the latest. If you can let us have the first few chapters in August, we can send them at once to Mr. Chromely, whom it is our intention to have illustrate the story, provided he can be got to do it."

The letter closed with a few formalities of an unimportant and stereotyped nature, and Harley immediately called at the office of Messrs. Herring, Beemer, & Chadwick, where, after learning that their best terms were no more unsatisfactory than publishers' best terms generally are, he accepted the commission.

And then, returning to his apartment, he went into what Kelly called one of his trances.

"He goes into one of his trances," Kelly had said, "hoists himself up to his little elevation, and peeps into the private life of hoi polloi until he strikes something worth putting down and the result he calls literature."

"Yes, and the people buy it, and read it, and call for more," said the Professor.

"Possibly because they love notoriety," said Kelly, "and they think if they call for more often enough, he will finally peep in at their key-holes and write them up. If he ever puts me into one of his books I'll waylay him at night and amputate his writing-hand."

"He won't," said the Professor. "I asked him once why he didn't, and he said you'd never do in one of his books, because you don't belong to real life at all. He thinks you are some new experiment of an enterprising Providence, and he doesn't want to use you until he sees how you turn out."

"He could put me down as I go," suggested the Doctor.

"That's so," replied the other. "I told him so, but he said he had no desire to write a lot of burlesque sketches containing no coherent idea."

"Oh, he said that, did he?" observed the Doctor, with a smile. "Well - wait till Stuart Harley comes to me for a prescription. I'll get even with him. I'll give him a pill, and he'll disappear - for ten days."

Whether it was as Kelly said or not, that Harley went into a trance and poked his nose into the private life of the people he wrote about, it was a fact that while meditating upon the possible output of his pen our author was as deaf to his surroundings as though he had departed into another world, and it rarely happened that his mind emerged from that condition without bringing along with it something of value to him in his work.

So it was upon this May morning. For an hour or two Harley lay quiescent, apparently gazing out of his flat window over the uninspiring chimney-pots of the City of New York, at the equally uninspiring Long Island station on the far side of the East River. It was well for him that his eye was able to see, and yet not see: forgetfulness of those smoking chimney-pots, the red-zincked roofs, the flapping under-clothing of the poorer than he, hung out to dry on the tenement tops, was essential to the construction of such a story as Messrs. Herring, Beemer, & Chadwick had in mind; and Harley successfully forgot them, and, coming back to consciousness, brought with him the dramatis personae of his story - and, taken as a whole, they were an interesting lot. The hero was like most of those gentlemen who live their little lives in the novels of the day, only Harley had modified his accomplishments in certain directions. Robert Osborne - such was his name - was not the sort of man to do impossible things for his heroine. He was not reckless. He was not a D'Artagnan lifted from the time of Louis the Fourteenth to the dull, prosaic days of President Faure. He was not even a Frenchman, but an essentially American American, who desires to know, before he does anything, why he does it, and what are his chances of success. I am not sure that if he had happened to see her struggling in the ocean he would have jumped in to rescue the young woman to whom his hand was plighted - I do not speak of his heart, for I am not Harley, and I do not know whether or not Harley intended that Osborne should be afflicted with so inconvenient an organ - I am not sure, I say, that if he had seen his best-beloved struggling in the ocean Osborne would have jumped in to rescue her without first stopping to remove such of his garments as might impede his progress back to land again. In short, he was not one of those impetuous heroes that we read about so often and see so seldom; but, taken altogether, he was sufficiently attractive to please the American girl who might be expected to read Harley's book; for that was one of the stipulations of Messrs. Herring, Beemer, & Chadwick when they made their verbal agreement with Harley.

"Make it go with the girls, Harley," Mr. Chadwick had said. "Men haven't time to read anything but the newspapers in this country. Hit the girls, and your fortune is made."

Harley didn't exactly see how his fortune was going to be made on the best terms of Messrs. Herring, Beemer, & Chadwick, even if he hit the girls with all the force of a battering-ram, but he promised to keep the idea in mind, and remained in his trance a trifle longer than might otherwise have been necessary, endeavoring to select the unquestionably correct hero for his story, and Osborne was the result. Osborne was moderately witty. His repartee smacked somewhat of the refined comic paper - that is to say, it was smart and cynical, and not always suited to the picture; but it wasn't vulgar or dull, and his personal appearance was calculated to arouse the liveliest interest. He was clean shaven and clean cut. He looked more like a modern ideal of infallible genius than Byron, and had probably played football and the banjo in college - Harley did not go back that far with him - all of which, it must be admitted, was pretty well calculated to assure the fulfilment of Harley's promise that the man should please the American girl. Of course the story was provided with a villain also, but he was a villain of a mild type. Mild villany was an essential part of Harley's literary creed, and this particular person was not conceived in heresy. His name was to have been Horace Balderstone, and with him Harley intended to introduce a lively satire on the employment, by certain contemporary writers, of the supernatural to produce dramatic effects. Balderstone was of course to be the rival of Osborne. In this respect Harley was commonplace; to his mind the villain always had to be the rival of the hero, just as in opera the tenor is always virtuous at heart if not otherwise, and the baritone a scoundrel, which in real life is not an invariable rule by any means. Indeed, there have been many instances in real life where the villain and the hero have been on excellent terms, and to the great benefit of the hero too. But in this case Balderstone was to follow in the rut, and become the rival of Osborne for the hand of Marguerite Andrews - the heroine. Balderstone was to write a book, which for a time should so fascinate Miss Andrews that she would be blind to the desirability of Osborne as a husband-elect; a book full of the weird and thrilling, dealing with theosophy and spiritualism, and all other "Tommyrotisms," as Harley called them, all of which, of course, was to be the making and the undoing of Balderstone; for equally of course, in the end, he would become crazed by the use of opium - the inevitable end of writers of that stamp. Osborne would rescue Marguerite from his fatal influence, and the last chapter would end with Marguerite lying pale and wan upon her sick-bed, recovering from the mental prostration which the influence over hers of a mind like Balderstone's was sure to produce, holding Osborne's hand in hers, and "smiling a sweet recognition at the lover to whose virtues she had so long been blind." Osborne would murmur, "At last!" and the book would close with a "first kiss," followed closely by six or eight pages of advertisements of other publications of Messrs. Herring, Beemer, & Chadwick. I mention the latter to show how thoroughly realistic Harley was. He thought out his books so truly and so fully before he sat down to write them that he seemed to see each written, printed, made and bound before him, a concrete thing from cover to cover.

Besides Osborne and Balderstone and Miss Andrews - of whom I shall at this time not speak at length, since the balance of this little narrative is to be devoted to the setting forth of her peculiarities and charms - there were a number of minor characters, not so necessary to the story perhaps as they might have been, but interesting enough in their way, and very well calculated to provide the material needed for the filling out of the required number of pages. Furthermore, they completed the picture.

"I don't want to put in three vivid figures, and leave the reader to imagine that the rest of the world has been wiped out of existence," said Harley, as he talked it over with me. "That is not art. There should be three types of character in every book - the positive, the average, and the negative. In that way you grade your story off into the rest of the world, and your reader feels that while he may never have met the positive characters, he has met the average or the negative, or both, and is therefore by one of these links connected with the others, and that gives him a personal interest in the story; and it's the reader's personal interest that the writer is after."

So Miss Andrews was provided with a very conventional aunt - the kind of woman you meet with everywhere; most frequently in church squabbles and hotel parlors, however. Mrs. Corwin was this lady's name, and she was to enact the role of chaperon to Miss Andrews. With Mrs. Corwin, by force of circumstances, came a pair of twin children, like those in the Heavenly Twins, only more real, and not so Sarah Grandiose in their manners and wit.

These persons Harley booked for the steamship New York, sailing from New York City for Southampton on the third day of July, 1895. The action was to open at that time, and Marguerite Andrews was to meet Horace Balderstone on that vessel on the evening of the second day out, with which incident the interest of Harley's story was to begin. But Harley had counted without his heroine. The rest of his cast were safely stowed away on ship-board and ready for action at the appointed hour, but the heroine MISSED THE STEAMER BY THREE MINUTES, AND IT WAS ALL HARLEY'S OWN FAULT.

CHAPTER II

A PRELIMINARY TRIAL

"I'll not be made a soft and dull-eyed fool
To shake the head, relent, and sigh, and yield."

"MERCHANT OF VENICE."

The extraordinary failure of Miss Andrews, cast for a star role in Stuart Harley's tale of Love and Villany, to appear upon the stage selected by the author for her debut, must be explained. As I have already stated at the close of the preceding chapter, it was entirely Harley's own fault. He had studied Miss Andrews too superficially to grasp thoroughly the more refined subtleties of her nature, and he found out, at a moment when it was too late to correct his error, that she was not a woman to be slighted in respect to the conventionalities of polite life, however trifling to a man of Harley's stamp these might seem to be. She was a stickler for form; and when she was summoned to go on board of an ocean steamship there to take part in a romance for the mere aggrandizement of a young author, she intended that he should not ignore the proprieties, even if in a sense the proprieties to which she referred did antedate the period at which his story was to open. She was willing to appear, but it seemed to her that Stuart Harley ought to see to it that she was escorted to the scene of action with the ceremony due to one of her position.

"What does he take me for?" she asked of Mrs. Corwin, indignantly, on the eve of her departure. "Am I a mere marionette, to obey his slightest behest, and at a moment's notice? Am I to dance when Stuart Harley pulls the string?"

"Not at all, my dear Marguerite," said Mrs. Corwin, soothingly. "If he thought that, he would not have selected you for his story. I think you ought to feel highly complimented that Mr. Harley should choose you for one of his books, and for such a conspicuous part, too. Look at me; do I complain? Am I holding out for the proprieties? And yet what is my situation? I'm simply dragged in by the hair; and my poor children, instead of having a nice, noisy Fourth of July at the sea-shore, must needs be put upon a great floating caravansary, to suffer seasickness and the other discomforts of ocean travel, so as to introduce a little juvenile fun into this great work of Mr. Harley's - and yet I bow my head meekly and go. Why? Because I feel that, inconspicuous though I shall be, nevertheless I am highly honored that Mr. Harley should select me from among many for the uses of his gifted pen."

"You are prepared, then," retorted Marguerite, "to place yourself unreservedly in Mr. Harley's hands? Shall you flirt with the captain if he thinks your doing so will add to the humorous or dramatic interest of his story? Will you permit your children to make impertinent remarks to every one aboard ship; to pick up sailors' slang and use it at the dining-table - in short, to make themselves obnoxiously clever at all times, in order that Mr. Harley's critics may say that his book fairly scintillates with wit, and gives gratifying evidence that 'the rising young author' has made a deep and careful analysis of the juvenile heart?"

"Mr. Harley is too much of a gentleman, Marguerite, to place me and my children in a false or ridiculous light," returned Mrs. Corwin, severely. "And even if he were not a gentleman, he is too true a realist to make me do anything which in the nature of things I should not do - which disposes of your entirely uncalled-for remark about the captain and myself. As for the children, Tommie would not repeat sailors' lingo at the table under any circumstances, and Jennie will not make herself obnoxiously clever at any time, because she has been brought up too carefully to fail to respect her elders. Both she and Tommie understand themselves thoroughly; and when Mr. Harley understands them, which he cannot fail to do after a short acquaintance, he will draw them as they are; and if previous to his complete understanding of their peculiarities he introduces into his story something foreign to their natures and obnoxious to me, their mother, I have no doubt he will correct his error when he comes to read the proofs of his story and sees his mistake."

"You have great confidence in Stuart Harley," retorted Miss Andrews, gazing out of the window with a pensive cast of countenance.

"Haven't you?" asked Mrs. Corwin, quickly.

"As a man, yes," returned Marguerite. "As an author, however, I think he is open to criticism. He is not always true to the real. Look at Lord Barncastle, in his study of

English manners! Barncastle, as he drew him, was nothing but a New York society man with a title, living in England. That is to say, he talked like an American, thought like one - there was no point of difference between them."

"And why should there be?" asked Mrs. Corwin. "If a New York society man is generally a weak imitation of an English peer - and no one has ever denied that such is the case - why shouldn't an English peer be represented as a sort of intensified New York society man?"

"Besides," said Miss Andrews, ignoring Mrs. Corwin's point, "I don't care to be presented too really to the reading public, especially on board a ship. I never yet knew a woman who looked well the second day out, and if I were to be presented as I always am the second day out, I should die of mortification. My hair goes out of curl, my face is the color of an unripe peach, and if I do go up on deck it is because I am so thoroughly miserable that I do not care who sees me or what the world thinks of me. I think it is very inconsiderate of Mr. Harley to open his story on an ocean steamer; and, what is more, I don't like the American line. Too many Americans of the brass-band type travel on it. Stuart Harley said so himself in his last book of foreign travel; but he sends me out on it just the same, and expects me to be satisfied. Perhaps he thinks I like that sort of American. If he does, he's got more imagination than he ever showed in his books."

"You must get to the other side in some way," said Mrs. Corwin. "It is at Venice that the trouble with Balderstone is to come, and that Osborne topples him over into the Grand Canal, and rescues you from his baleful influence."

"Humph!" said Marguerite, with a scornful shrug of her shoulders. "Robert Osborne! A likely sort of person to rescue me from anything! He wouldn't have nerve enough to rescue me from a grasshopper if he were armed to the teeth. Furthermore, I shall not go to Venice in August. It's bad enough in April - damp and hot - the home of malaria - an asylum for artistic temperaments; and insecty. No, my dear aunt, even if I overlook everything else to please Mr. Harley, he'll have to modify the Venetian part of that story, for I am determined that no pen of his shall force me into Italy at this season. I wouldn't go there to please Shakespeare, much less Stuart Harley. Let the affair come off at Interlaken, if it is to come off at all, which I doubt."

"There is no Grand Canal at Interlaken," said Mrs. Corwin, sagely; for she had been an omnivorous reader of Baedeker since she had learned the part she was to play in Harley's book, and was therefore well up in geography.

"No; but there's the Jungfrau. Osborne can push Balderstone down the side of an Alp and kill him," returned Miss Andrews, viciously.

"Why, Marguerite! How can you talk so? Mr. Harley doesn't wish to have Balderstone killed," cried Mrs. Corwin, aghast. "If Osborne killed Balderstone he'd be a murderer, and they'd execute him."

"Which is exactly what I want," said Miss Andrews, firmly. "If he lives, it pleases the omnipotent Mr. Harley that I shall marry him, and I positively - Well, just you wait and see."

There was silence for some minutes.

"Then I suppose you will decline to go abroad altogether?" asked Mrs. Corwin after a while; "and Mr. Harley will be forced to get some one else; and I - I shall be deprived of a pleasant tour - because I'm only to be one of the party because I'm your aunt."

Mrs. Corwin's lip quivered a little as she spoke. She had anticipated much pleasure from her trip.

"No, I shall not decline to go," Miss Andrews replied. "I expect to go, but it is entirely on your account. I must say, however, that Stuart Harley will find out, to his sorrow, that I am not a doll, to be worked with a string. I shall give him a scare at the outset which will show him that I know the rights of a heroine, and that he must respect them. For instance, he cannot ignore my comfort. Do you suppose that because his story is to open with my beautiful self on board that ship, I'm to be there without his making any effort to get me there? Not I! You and the children and Osborne and Balderstone may go down any way you please. You may go on the elevated railroad or on foot. You may go on the horse-cars, or you may go on the luggage-van. It is immaterial to me what you do; but when it comes to myself, Stuart Harley must provide a carriage, or I miss the boat. I don't wish to involve you in this. You want to go, and are willing to go in his way, which simply means turning up at the right moment, with no trouble to him. From your point of view it is all right. You are anxious to go abroad, and are grateful to Mr. Harley for letting you go. For me, however, he must do differently. I have no particular desire to leave America, and if I go at all it is as a favor to him, and he must act accordingly. It is a case of carriage or no heroine. If I'm left behind, you and the rest can go along without me. I shall do very well, and it will be Mr. Harley's own fault. It may hurt his story somewhat, but that is no concern of mine."

"I suppose the reason why he doesn't send a carriage is that that part of your life doesn't appear in his story," explained Mrs. Corwin.

"That doesn't affect the point that he ought to send one," said Marguerite. "He needn't write up the episode of the ride to the pier unless he wants to, but the fact remains that it's his duty to see me safely on board from my home, and that he shall do, or I fail him at the moment he needs me. If he is selfish enough to overlook the matter, he must suffer the consequences."

All of which, I think, was very reasonable. No heroine likes to feel that she is called into being merely to provide copy for the person who is narrating her story; and to be impressed with the idea that the moment she is off the stage she must shift entirely for herself is too humiliating to be compatible with true heroism.

Now it so happened that in his meditations upon that opening chapter the scene of which was to be placed on board of the New York, Stuart realized that his story of Miss Andrews's character had indeed been too superficial. He found that out at the moment he sat down to describe her arrival at the pier, as it would be in all likelihood. What would she say the moment she - the moment she what? - the moment she "emerged from the perilous stream of vehicles which crowd West Street from morning until night," or the moment "she stepped out of the cab as it drew up at the foot of the gangway"? That was the point. How would she arrive - on foot or in a cab? Which way would she come, and at what time must she start from home? Should she come alone, or should Mrs. Corwin and the twins come with her? - or would a woman of her stamp not be likely to have an intimate friend to accompany her to the steamer? Stuart was a rapid thinker, and as he pondered over these problems it did not take him long to reach the conclusion that a cab was necessary for Miss Andrews; and that Mrs. Corwin and the twins, with Osborne and Balderstone, might get aboard in their own way. He also decided that it would be an excellent plan to have Marguerite's old school friend Mrs. Willard accompany her to the steamer. By an equally rapid bit of thought he concluded that if the cab started from the Andrews apartment at Fifty-ninth Street and Central Park at 9.30 A.M., the trip to the pier could easily be made in an hour, which would be in ample time, since the sailing hour of the New York was eleven. Unfortunately Harley, in his hurry, forgot two or three incidents of departures generally, especially departures of women, which he should not have overlooked. It was careless of him to forget that a woman about to travel abroad wants to make herself as stunning as she possibly can on the day of departure, so that the impression she will make at the start shall be strong enough to carry her through the dowdy stage which comes, as Marguerite had intimated, on the second and third days at sea; and to expect a woman like Marguerite Andrews, who really had no responsibilities to call her up at an early hour, to be ready at 9.30 sharp, was a fatal error, unless he provided his cab with an unusually fast horse, or a pair of horses, both of which Harley neglected to do. Miss Andrews was twenty minutes late at starting the first time, and just a half-hour behind schedule time when, having rushed back to her rooms for her gloves, which in the excitement of the moment she had forgotten, she started finally for the ship. Even then all would have been well had the unfortunate author not overlooked one other vital point. Instead of sending the cab straight down Fifth Avenue, to Broadway, to Barclay Street, he sent it down Sixth, and thence through Greenwich Village, emerging at West Street at its junction with Christopher, and then the inevitable happened.

THE CAB WAS BLOCKED!

"I had no idea it was so far," said Marguerite, looking out of the cab window at the crowded and dirty thoroughfare.

"It's a good mile farther yet," replied Mrs. Willard. "I shall have just that much more of your society."

"It looks to me," said Marguerite, with a short laugh, as the cab came suddenly to a halt -"it looks to me as if you were likely to have more than that of it; for we are in an apparently inextricable, immovable mixture of trucks, horse-cars, and incompetent policemen, and nothing short of a miracle will get us a mile farther along in twenty minutes."

"I do believe you are right," said Mrs. Willard, looking at her watch anxiously. "What will you do if you miss the steamer?"

"Escape a horrid fate," laughed Marguerite, gayly.

"Poor Mr. Harley - why, it will upset his whole story," said Mrs. Willard.

"And save his reputation," said Marguerite. "It wouldn't have been real, that story," she added. "In the first place, Balderstone couldn't write a story that would fascinate me; he could never acquire a baleful influence over me; and, finally, I never should marry Robert Osborne under any circumstances. He's not at all the style of man I admire. I'm willing to go along and let Mr. Harley try to work it out his way, but he will give it up as a bad idea before long - if I catch the steamer; and if I don't, then he'll have to modify the story. That modified, I'm willing to be his heroine."

"But your aunt and the twins - they must be aboard by this time. They will be worried to death about you," suggested Mrs. Willard.

"For a few moments - but Aunt Emma wanted to go, and she and the rest of them will have a good time, I've no doubt," replied Miss Andrews, calmly; and here Stuart Harley's heroine actually chuckled. "And maybe Mr. Harley can make a match between Aunt Emma and Osborne, which will suit the publishers and please the American girl," she said, gleefully. "I almost hope we do miss it."

And miss it they did, as I have already told you, by three minutes. As the cab entered the broad pier, the great steamer moved slowly but surely out into the stream, and Mrs. Willard and Mr. Harley's heroine were just in time to see Mrs. Corwin wildly waving her parasol at the captain on the bridge, beseeching him in agonized tones to go back just for a moment, while two separate and distinct twins, one male and one female, peered over the rail, weeping bitterly. Incidentally mention may be made of two young men, Balderstone and Osborne, who sat chatting gayly together in the smoking-room.

"Well, Osborne," said one, lighting his cigar, "she didn't arrive."

"No," smiled the other. "Fact is, Balderstone, I'm glad of it. She's too snippy for me, and I'm afraid I should have quarrelled with you about her in a half-hearted, unconvincing manner."

"I'm afraid I'd have been the same," rejoined Balderstone; "for, between us, there's a pretty little brunette from Chicago up on deck, and Marguerite Andrews would have got little attention from me while she was about, unless Harley violently outraged my feelings and his own convictions."

And so the New York sailed out to sea, and Marguerite Andrews watched her from the pier until she had faded from view.

As for Stuart Harley, the author, he sat in his study, wringing his hands and cursing his carelessness.

"I'll have to modify the whole story now," he said, impatiently, "since it is out of my power to bring the New York back into port, with my hero, villain, chaperon, and twins; but whenever or wherever the new story may be laid, Marguerite Andrews shall be the heroine - she interests me. Meantime let Mrs. Willard chaperon her."

And closing his manuscript book with a bang, Harley lit a cigarette, put on his hat, and went to the club.

CHAPTER III

THE RECONSTRUCTION BEGINS

"Then gently scan your brother man,
Still gentler sister woman;
Tho' they may gang a kennin wrang,
To step aside is human."

                                        BURNS.

When, a few days later, Harley came to the reconstruction of his story, he began to appreciate the fact that what had seemed at first to be his misfortune was, on the whole, a matter for congratulation; and as he thought over the people he had sent to sea, he came to rejoice that Marguerite was not one of the party.

"Osborne wasn't her sort, after all," he mused to himself that night over his coffee. "He hadn't much mind. I'm afraid I banked too much on his good looks, and too little upon what I might call her independence; for of all the heroines I ever had, she is the most sufficient unto herself. Had she gone along I'm half afraid I couldn't have got rid of Balderstone so easily either, for he's a determined devil as I see him; and his intellectual qualities were so vastly superior to those of Osborne that by mere contrast they would most certainly have appealed to her strongly. The baleful influence might have affected her seriously, and Osborne was never the man to overcome it, and strict realism would have forced her into an undesirable marriage. Yes, I'm glad it turned out the way it did; she's too good for either of them. I couldn't have done the tale as I intended without a certain amount of compulsion, which would never have worked out well. She'd have been miserable with Osborne for a husband anyhow, even if he did succeed in outwitting Balderstone."

Then Harley went into a trance for a moment. From this he emerged almost immediately with a laugh. The travellers on the sea had come to his mind.

"Poor Mrs. Corwin," he said, "she's awfully upset. I shall have to give her some diversion. Let's see, what shall it be? She's a widow, young and fascinating. H'm - not a bad foundation for a romance. There must be a man on the ship who'd like her; but, hang it all! there are those twins. Not much romance for her with those twins along, unless the man's a fool; and she's too fine a woman for a fool. Men don't fall in love with whole families that way. Now if they had only been left on the pier with Miss Andrews, it would have worked up well. Mrs. Corwin could have fascinated some fellow-traveller, won his heart, accepted him at Southampton, and told him about the twins afterwards. As a test of his affection that would be a strong situation; but with the twins along, making the remarks they are likely to make, and all that - no, there is no hope for Mrs. Corwin, except in a juvenile story - something like 'Two Twins in a Boat, not to Mention the Widow,' or something of that sort. Poor woman! I'll let her rest in peace, for the present. She'll enjoy her trip, anyhow; and as for Osborne and

Balderstone, I'll let them fight it out for that dark-eyed little woman from Chicago I saw on board, and when the best man wins I'll put the whole thing into a short story."

Then began a new quest for characters to go with Marguerite Andrews.

"She must have a chaperon, to begin with," thought Harley. "That is indispensable. Herring, Beemer, & Chadwick regard themselves as conservators of public morals, in their 'Blue and Silver Series,' so a girl unmarried and without a chaperon would never do for this book. If they were to publish it in their 'Yellow Prism Series' I could fling all such considerations to the winds, for there they cater to stronger palates, palates cultivated by French literary cooks, and morals need not be considered, provided the story is well told and likely to sell; but this is for the other series, and a chaperon is a sine qua non. Marguerite doesn't need one half as much as the girls in the 'Yellow Prism' books, but she's got to have one just the same, or the American girl will not read about her: and who is better than Dorothy Willard, who has charge of her now?"

Harley slapped his knee with delight.

"How fortunate I'd provided her!" he said. "I've got my start already, and without having to think very hard over it either."

The trance began again, and lasted several hours, during which time Kelly and the Professor stole softly into Harley's rooms, and, perceiving his condition, respected it.

"He's either asleep or imagining," said the Professor, in a whisper. "He can't imagine," returned the Doctor. "Call it - realizing. Whatever it is he's up to, we mustn't interfere. There isn't any use waking him anyhow. I know where he keeps his cigars. Let's sit down and have a smoke."

This the intruders did, hoping that sooner or later their host would observe their presence; but Harley lay in blissful unconsciousness of their coming, and they finally grew weary of waiting.

"He must be at work on a ten-volume novel," said the Doctor. "Let's go."

And with that they departed. Night came on, and with it darkness, but Harley never moved. The fact was he was going through an examination of the human race to find a man good enough for Marguerite Andrews, and it speaks volumes for the interest she had suddenly inspired in his breast that it took him so long to find what he wanted.

Along about nine o'clock he gave a deep sigh and returned to earth.

"I guess I've got him," he said, wearily, rubbing his forehead, which began to ache a trifle. "I'll model him after the Professor. He's a good fellow, moderately good-looking, has position, and certainly knows something, as professors go. I doubt if he is imposing enough for the American girl generally, but he's the best I can get in the time at my disposal."

So the Professor was unconsciously slated for the office of hero; Mrs. Willard was cast for chaperon, and the

Doctor, in spite of Harley's previous resolve not to use him, was to be introduced for the comedy element. The villain selected was the usual poverty-stricken foreigner with a title and a passion for wealth, which a closer study of his heroine showed Harley that Miss Andrews possessed; for on her way home from the pier she took Mrs. Willard to the Amsterdam and treated her to a luncheon which nothing short of a ten-dollar bill would pay for, after which the two went shopping, replenishing Miss Andrews's wardrobe - most of which lay snugly stored in the hold of the New York, and momentarily getting farther and farther away from its fair owner - in the course of which tour Miss Andrews expended a sum which, had Harley possessed it, would have made it unnecessary for him to write the book he had in mind at all.

"It's good she's rich," sighed Harley. "That will make it all the easier to have her go to Newport and attract the Count."

At the moment that Harley spoke these words to himself Mrs. Willard and Marguerite, accompanied by Mr. Willard, entered the mansion of the latter on Fifth Avenue. They had spent the afternoon and evening at the Andrews apartment, arranging for its closing until the return of Mrs. Corwin. Marguerite meanwhile was to be the guest of the Willards.

"Next week we'll run up to Newport," said Dorothy. "The house is ready, and Bob is going for his cruise."

Marguerite looked at her curiously for a moment.

"Did you intend to go there all along?" she asked.

"Yes - of course. Why do you ask?" returned Mrs. Willard.

"Why, that very idea came into my mind at the moment," replied Marguerite. "I thought this afternoon I'd run up to Riverdale and stay with the Hallidays next week, when all of a sudden Newport came into my mind, and it has been struggling there with Riverdale for two hours - until I almost began to believe somebody was trying to compel me to go to Newport. If it is your idea, and has been all along, I'll go; but if Stuart Harley is trying to get me down there for literary purposes, I simply shall not do it."

"You had better dismiss that idea from your mind at once, my dear," said Mrs. Willard. "Mr. Harley never compels. No compulsion is the corner-stone of his literary structure; free will is his creed: you may count on that. If he means to make you his heroine still, it will be at Newport if you are at Newport, at Riverdale if you happen to be at Riverdale. Do come with me, even if he does impress you as endeavoring to force you; for at Newport I shall be your chaperon, and I should dearly love to be put in a book - with you. Bob has asked Jack Perkins down, and Mrs. Howlett writes me that Count Bonetti, of Naples, is there, and is a really delightful fellow. We shall have -"

"You simply confirm my fears," interrupted Marguerite. "You are to be Harley's chaperon, Professor Perkins is his hero, and Count Bonetti is the villain -"

"Why, Marguerite, how you talk!" cried Mrs. Willard. "Do you exist merely in Stuart Harley's brain? Do I? Are we none of us living creatures to do as we will? Are we nothing more than materials pigeon-holed for Mr.

Harley's future use? Has Count Bonetti crossed the ocean just to please Mr. Harley?"

"I don't know what I believe," said Miss Andrews, "and I don't care much either way, as long as I have independence of action. I'll go with you, Dorothy; but if it turns out, as I fear, that we are expected to act our parts in a Harley romance, that romance will receive a shock from which it will never recover."

"Why do you object so to Mr. Harley, anyhow? I thought you liked his books," said Mrs. Willard.

"I do; some of them," Marguerite answered; "and I like him; but he does not understand me, and until he does he shall not put me in his stories. I'll rout him at every point, until he -"

Marguerite paused. Her face flushed. Tears came into her eyes.

"Until he what, dearest?" asked Mrs. Willard, sympathetically.

"I don't know," said Marguerite, with a quiver in her voice, as she rose and left the room.

"I fancy we'd better go at once, Bob," said Mrs. Willard to her husband, later on. "Marguerite is quite upset by the experiences of the day, and New York is fearfully hot."

"I agree with you," returned Willard. "Jerrold sent word this afternoon that the boat will be ready Friday, instead of Thursday of next week; so if you'll pack up to-morrow we can board her Friday, and go up the Sound by water instead of by rail. It will be pleasanter for all hands."

Which was just what Harley wanted. The Willards were of course not conscious of the fact, though Mrs. Willard's sympathy with Marguerite led her to suspect that such was the case; for that such was the case was what Marguerite feared.

"We are being forced, Dorothy," she said, as she stepped on the yacht two days later.

"Well, what if we are? It's pleasanter going this way than by rail, isn't it?" Mrs. Willard replied, with some impatience. "If we owe all this to Stuart Harley, we ought to thank him for his kindness. According to your theory he could have sent us up on a hot, dusty train, and had a collision ready for us at New London, in order to kill off a few undesirable characters and give his hero a chance to distinguish himself. I think that even from your own point of view Mr. Harley is behaving in a very considerate fashion."

"No doubt you think so," returned Marguerite, spiritedly. "But it's different with you. You are settled in life. Your husband is the man of your choice; you are happy, with everything you want. You will do nothing extraordinary in the book. If you did do something extraordinary you would cease to be a good chaperon, and from that moment would be cast aside; but I - I am in a different position altogether. I am a single woman, unsettled as yet, for whom this author in his infinite wisdom deems it necessary to provide a lover and husband; and in order that his narrative of how I get this person he has selected - without consulting my tastes - may interest a lot of other girls, who are expected to buy and read his book, he makes me the object of an intriguing fortune-hunter from Italy. I am to believe he is a real nobleman, and all that; and a stupid wiseacre from the York University, who can't dance, and who thinks of nothing but his books and his club, is to come in at the right moment and expose the Count, and all such trash as that. I know at the outset how it all is to be. You couldn't deceive a sensible girl five minutes with Count Bonetti, any more than that Balderstone man, who is now making a useless trip across the Atlantic with my aunt and her twins, could have exerted a 'baleful influence' over me with his diluted spiritualism. I'm not an idiot, my dear Dorothy."

"You are a heroine, love," returned Mrs. Willard.

"Perhaps - but I am the kind of heroine who would stop a play five minutes after the curtain had risen on the first act if the remaining four acts depended on her failing to see something that was plain to the veriest dolt in the audience," Marguerite replied, with spirit. "Nobody shall ever write me up save as I am."

"Well - perhaps you are wrong this time. Perhaps Mr. Harley isn't going to make a book of you," said Mrs. Willard.

"Very likely he isn't," said Marguerite; "but he's trying it - I know that much."

"And how, pray?" asked Mrs. Willard.

"That," said Marguerite, her frown vanishing and a smile taking its place - "that is for the present my secret. I'll tell you some day, but not until I have baffled Mr. Harley in his ill-advised purpose of marrying me off to a man I don't want, and wouldn't have under any circumstances.

Even if I had caught the New York the other day his plans would have miscarried. I'd never have married that Osborne man; I'd have snubbed Balderstone the moment he spoke to me; and if Stuart Harley had got a book out of my trip to Europe at all, it would have been a series of papers on some such topic as 'The Spinster Abroad, or How to be Happy though Single.' No more shall I take the part he intends me to in this Newport romance, unless he removes Count Bonetti from the scene entirely, and provides me with a different style of hero from his Professor, the original of whom, by-the-way, as I happen to know, is already married and has two children. I went to school with his wife, and I know just how much of a hero he is."

And so they went to Newport, and Harley's novel opened swimmingly. His description of the yacht was perfect; his narration of the incidents of the embarkation could not be improved upon in any way. They were absolutely true to the life.

But his account of what Marguerite Andrews said and did and thought while on the Willards' yacht was not realism at all - it was imagination of the wildest kind, for she said, did, and thought nothing of the sort.

Harley did his best, but his heroine was obdurate, and the poor fellow did not know that he was writing untruths, for he verily believed that he heard and saw all that he attributed to her exactly as he put it down.

So the story began well, and Harley for a time was quite happy. At the end of a week, however, he had a fearful set-back. Count Bonetti was ready to be presented to Marguerite according to the plan, but there the schedule broke down.

Harley's heroine took a new and entirely unexpected tack.

CHAPTER IV

A CHAPTER FROM HARLEY, WITH NOTES

"Good-bye, proud world, I'm going home.
Thou art not my friend, and I'm not thine."

EMERSON.

I think the reader will possibly gain a better idea of what happened at the Howlett dance, at which Count Bonetti was to have been presented to Miss Andrews, if I forego the pleasure of writing this chapter myself, and produce instead the chapter of Stuart Harley's ill-fated book which was to have dealt with that most interesting incident. Having relinquished all hope of ever getting that particular story into shape without a change of heroine, and being unwilling to go to that extreme, Mr. Harley has very kindly placed his manuscript at my disposal.

"Use it as you will, my dear fellow," he said, when I asked him for it. "I can't do anything with it myself, and it is merely occupying space in my pigeon-holes for which I can find better use. It may need a certain amount of revision - in fact, it is sure to, for it is unconscionably long, and, thanks to the persistent failure of Miss Andrews to do as I thought she would, may frequently seem incoherent. For your own sake revise it, for the readers of your book won't believe that you are telling a true story anyhow; they will say that you wrote this chapter and attributed it to me, and you will find yourself held responsible for its shortcomings. I have inserted a few notes here and there which will give you an idea of what I suffered as I wrote on and found her growing daily less and less tractable, with occasionally an indication of the point of divergence between her actual behavior and that which I expected of her."

To a fellow-workman in literary fields this chapter is of pathetic interest, though it may not so appear to the reader who knows little of the difficulties of authorship. I can hardly read it myself without a feeling of most intense pity for poor Harley. I can imagine the sleepless nights which followed the shattering of his hopes as to what his story might be by the recalcitrant attitude of the young woman he had honored so highly by selecting her for his heroine. I can almost feel the bitter sense of disappointment, which must have burned to the very depths of his soul, when he finally realized how completely overturned were all his plans, and I cannot forego calling attention to the constancy to his creed of Stuart Harley, in sacrificing his opportunity rather than his principles, as shown by his resolute determination not to force Miss Andrews to do his bidding, even though it required merely the dipping of his pen into the ink and the resolution to do so.

I cannot blame her, however. Granting to Harley the right to a creed, Miss Andrews, too, it must be admitted, was entitled to have views as to how she ought to behave under given circumstances, and if she found her notions running counter to his, it was only proper that she should act according to the dictates of her own heart, or mind, or whatever else it may be that a woman reasons with, rather than according to his wishes.

As to all questions of this kind, however, as between the two, the reader must judge, and one document in evidence is Harley's chapter, which ran in this wise:

A MEETING

"Stop beating, heart, and in a moment calm
The question answer - is this, then, my fate?"
- PERKINS'S "Odes."

As the correspondents of the New York papers had surmised, invitations for the Howlett ball were issued on the 12th. It is not surprising that the correspondents in this instance should be guilty of that rare crime among society reporters, accuracy, for their information was derived from a perfectly reliable source, Mrs. Howlett's butler, in whose hands the addressing of the envelopes had been placed - a man of imposing presence, and of great value to the professional snappers-up of unconsidered trifles of social gossip in the pay of the Sunday newspapers, with many of whom he was on terms of closest intimacy. Of course Mrs. Howlett was not aware that her household contained a personage of great journalistic importance, any more than her neighbor, Mrs. Floyd-Hopkins, was aware that it was her maid who had furnished the Weekly Journal of Society with the vivid account of the scandalous behavior, at her last dinner, of Major Pompoly, who had to be forcibly ejected from the Floyd-Hopkins domicile by the husband of Mrs. Jernigan Smith - a social morsel which attracted much attention several years ago. Every effort was made to hush that matter up, and the guests all swore eternal secrecy; but the Weekly Journal of Society had it, and, strangely enough, had it right, in its next issue; but the maid was never suspected, even though she did appear to be possessed of more ample means than usual for some time after. Mrs. Floyd-Hopkins preferred to suspect one of her guests, and, on the whole, was not sorry that the matter had got abroad, for everybody talked about it, and through the episode her dinner became one of the historic banquets of the season.

The Willards, who were by this time comfortably settled at "The Needles," their cottage on the cliff, it is hardly necessary to state, were among those invited, and with their cards was included one for Marguerite. Added to the card was a personal note from Mrs. Howlett to Miss Andrews, expressing the especial hope that she would not fail them, all of which was very gratifying to the young girl.

"See what I've got," she cried, gleefully, running into Mrs. Willard's "den" at the head of the beautiful oaken stairs.

(Note. - At this point in Harley's manuscript there is evidence of indecision on the author's part. His heroine had begun to bother him a trifle. He had written a half-dozen lines descriptive of Miss Andrews's emotions at receiving a special note of invitation, subsequently erasing them. The word "gleefully" had been scratched out, and then restored in place of "scornfully," which had at first been substituted for it. It was plain that Harley was not quite certain as to how much a woman of Miss Andrews's type would care for a special attention of this nature, even if she cared for it at all. As a matter of fact, the word chosen should have been "dubiously," and neither "gleefully" nor "scornfully"; for the real truth was that there was no reason why Mrs. Howlett should so honor Marguerite, and the girl at once began to wonder if it were not an extra precaution of Harley's to assure her presence at the ball for the benefit of himself and his publishers. The author finally wrote it as I have given it above, however, and Miss Andrews received her special invitation "gleefully" - according to Harley. He perceives her doubt, however, without comprehending it; for after describing Mrs. Willard's reading of the note, he goes on.)

"That is very nice of Mrs. Howlett," said Mrs. Willard, handing Marguerite back her note. "It is a special honor, my dear, by which you should feel highly flattered. She doesn't often do things like that."

"I should think not," said Marguerite. "I am a perfect stranger to her, and that she should do it at all strikes me as being most extraordinary. It doesn't seem sincere, and I can't help thinking that some extraneous circumstance has been brought to bear upon her to force her to do it."

(Note. - Stuart Harley has commented upon this as follows: "As I read this over I must admit that Miss Andrews was right. Why I had Mrs. Howlett do such a thing I don't know, unless it was that my own admiration for my heroine led me to believe that some more than usual attention was her due. In my own behalf I will say that I should in all probability have eliminated or corrected this false note when I came to the revision of my proofs." The chapter then proceeds.)

"What shall we wear?" mused Mrs. Willard, as Marguerite folded Mrs. Howlett's note and replaced it in its envelope.

"I must positively decline to discuss that question. It is of no public interest," snapped Marguerite, her face flushing angrily. "My clothing is my own business, and no one's else." She paused a moment, and then, in an apologetic tone, she added, "I'd be perfectly willing to talk with you about it generally, my dear Dorothy, but not now."

Mrs. Willard looked at the girl in surprise.

(Note. - Stuart Harley has written this in the margin: "Here you have one of the situations which finally compelled me to relinquish this story. You know yourself how hard it is to make 30,000 words out of a slight situation, and at the same time stick to probability. I had an idea, in mapping out this chapter, that I could make three or four interesting pages - interesting to the girls, mind you - out of a discussion of what they should wear at the Howlett dance. It was a perfectly natural subject for discussion at the time and under the circumstances. It would have been a good thing in the book, too, for it might have conveyed a few wholesome hints in the line of good taste in dress which would have made my story of some value. Women are always writing to the papers, asking, 'What shall I wear here?' and 'What shall I wear there?' The ideas of two women like Mrs. Willard and Marguerite Andrews would have been certain to be interesting, elevating, and exceedingly useful to such people, but the moment I attempted to involve them in that discussion Miss Andrews declined utterly to speak, and I was cut out of some six or seven hundred quite important words. I had supposed all women alike in that matter, but I find I was mistaken; one, at least, won't discuss clothes - but I don't wonder that Mrs. Willard looked up in surprise. I put that in just to please myself, for of course the whole incident would have had to be cut out when the manuscript went to the type-setter." The chapter takes a new lead here, as follows:)

Mrs. Willard was punctiliously prompt in sending the acceptances of herself and Mr. Willard to Mrs. Howlett, and at the same time Marguerite's acceptance was despatched, although she was at first disposed to send her regrets. She was only moderately fond of those inconsequent pleasures which make the life social. She was a good dancer, but a more excellent talker, and she preferred talking to dancing; but the inanity of what are known as stair talks at dances oppressed her; nor did she look forward with any degree of pleasure to what we might term conservatory confidences, which in these luxurious days have become so large a factor in terpsichorean diversions, for Marguerite was of a practical nature. She had once chilled the heart of a young poet by calling Venice malarious (Harley little realized when he wrote this how he would have suffered had he carried out his original intention and transplanted Marguerite to the City of the Sea!), and a conservatory to her was a thing for mid-day, and not for midnight. She was therefore not particularly anxious to spend an evening - which began at an aggravatingly late hour instead of at a reasonable time, thanks to a social custom which has its foundation in nothing short of absolute insanity - in the pursuit of nothing of greater value than dancing, stair talks, and conservatory confidences; but Mrs. Willard soon persuaded her that she ought to go, and go she did.

It was a beautiful night, that of the 22d of July. Newport was at her best. The morning had been oppressively warm, but along about three in the afternoon a series of short and sharp electrical storms came, and as quickly went, cooling the heated city, and freshening up the air until it was as clear as crystal, and refreshing as a draught of cold spring-water.

At the Howlett mansion on Bellevue Avenue all was in readiness for the event. The caterer's wagons had arrived with their dainty contents, and had gone, and now the Hungarian band was sending forth over the cool night air those beautiful and weird waves of melody which entrance the most unwilling ear. About the broad and spacious grounds festooned lights hung from tree to tree; here and there little rose-scented bowers for tete-a-tete talks were set; from within, streaming through the windows in regal beauty, came the lights of the vast ballroom, the reception-rooms, and the beautifully designed dining-hall - lately added by young Morris Black, the architect, to Mrs. Howlett's already perfect house.

On the ballroom floor are some ten or twenty couples gracefully waltzing to the strains of Sullivan, and in the midst of these we see Marguerite Andrews threading her way across the room with some difficulty, attended by Mr. and Mrs. Willard. They have just arrived. As Marguerite walks across the hall she attracts every one. There is that about her which commands attention. At the instant of her entrance Count Bonetti is on the qui Vive.

"Py Chove!" he cries, as he leans gracefully against the doorway opening into the conservatory. "Zare, my dear friend, zat iss my idea of ze truly peautiful woman. Vat iss her name?"

"That is Miss Andrews of New York, Count," the person addressed replies. "She is up here with the Willards."

"I musd meed her," says the Count, his eye following Marguerite as she walks up to Mrs. Howlett and is greeted effusively by that lady.

Marguerite is pale, and appears anxious. Even to the author the ways of the women in his works are inscrutable; so upon this occasion. She is pale, but I cannot say why. Can it be that she has an intuitive knowledge that to-night may decide her whole future life? Who can tell? Woman's intuitions are great, and there be those who say they are unerringly true. One by one, with the exception of Count Bonetti, the young men among Mrs. Howlett's guests are presented - Bonetti prefers to await a more favorable opportunity - and to all Marguerite appears to be the beautiful woman she is. Hers is an instant success. A new beauty has dawned upon the Newport horizon.

Let us describe her as she stands.

(Note. - There is a blank space left here. At first I thought it was because Harley wished to reflect a little before drawing a picture of so superb a woman as he seemed to think her, and go on to the conclusion of the chapter, the main incidents being hot in his mind, and the purely descriptive matters more easily left to calmer moments. He informs me, however, that such was not the case. "When I came to describe her as she stood," he said, "she had disappeared, and I had to search all over the house before I finally found her in the conservatory. So I changed the chapter to read thus:")

After a half-hour of dancing and holding court - for Marguerite's triumph was truly that of a queen, it was so complete - Miss Andrews turned to Mr. Willard and took his arm.

"Let us go into the conservatory," she said, in a whisper. "I have heard so much about Mrs. Howlett's orchids, I should like to see them."

Willard, seeing that she was tired and slightly bored by the incessant chatter of those about her, escorted her out through the broad door into the conservatory. As she passed from the ballroom the dark eyes of Count Bonetti flashed upon her, but she heeded them not, moving on into the floral bower in apparently serene unconsciousness of that person's presence. Here Willard got her a chair.

"Will you have an ice?" he asked, as she seated herself beneath one of the lofty palms.

"Yes," she answered, simply. "I can wait here alone if you will get it."

Willard passed out, and soon returned with the ice; but as he came through the doorway Bonetti stopped him and whispered something in his ear.

"Certainly, Count, right away," Willard answered. "Come along."

Bonetti needed no second bidding, but followed Willard closely, and soon stood expectant before Marguerite.

"Miss Andrews," said Willard, "may I have the pleasure of presenting Count Bonetti?"

The Count's head nearly collided with his toes in the bow that he made.

"Mr. Willard," returned Miss Andrews, coldly, ignoring

the Count, "feeling as I do that Count Bonetti is merely a bogus Count with acquisitive instincts, brought here, like myself, for literary purposes of which I cannot approve, I must reply to your question that you may not have that pleasure."

With which remark (concludes Stuart Harley) Miss Marguerite Andrews swept proudly from the room, ordered her carriage, and went home, thereby utterly ruining the second story of her life that I had undertaken to write. But I shall make one more effort.

CHAPTER V

AN EXPERIMENT

"And thus I'll curb her mad and headstrong humor.
He that knows better how to tame a shrew,
Now let him speak; 'tis charity to show."

"TAMING OF THE SHREW."

"What would have happened if shc had behaved differently, Stuart?" I asked, after I had read the pages he had so kindly placed at my disposal.

"Oh, nothing in particular to which she could reasonably object," returned Harley. "The incidents of a truly realistic novel are rarely objectionable, except to people of a captious nature. I intended to have Bonetti dance attendance upon Miss Andrews for the balance of the season, that's all, hoping thereby to present a good picture of life at Newport in July and part of August. About the middle of August I was going to transport the whole cast to Bar Harbor, for variety's sake. That would have been another opportunity to get a good deal of the American summer atmosphere into the book. I wish I could afford the kind of summer I contemplated giving her."

"You didn't intend that she should fall in love with Bonetti?" I asked.

"Not to any serious extent," said Harley, deprecatingly. "Even if she had a little, she'd have come out of it all right as soon as the hero turned up, and she had a chance to see the difference between a manly man of her own country and a little titled fortune hunter from the land of macaroni. Bonetti wasn't to be a bad fellow at all. He was merely an Italian, which he couldn't help, being born so, and therefore, as she said, of an acquisitive nature. There is no villany in that, however - that is, no reprehensible villany. He was after a rich marriage because he was fond of a life of ease. She'd have found him amusing, at any rate."

"But he was bogus!" I suggested.

"Not at all," said Harley, impatiently. "That's what vexes me more than anything else. She made a very bad mistake there. As a Count, Bonetti was quite as real as his financial necessities."

"It was a beastly awkward situation, that conservatory scene," said I. "Especially for Willard. The Count might have challenged him. What became of the Count when it was over?"

"I don't know," said Harley. "I left him to get out of his predicament as best he could. Possibly he did challenge Willard. I haven't taken the trouble to find out. If, as I think, however, he's a living person, he'll extricate himself from his difficulty all right; if he's not, and I have unwittingly allowed myself to conjure him up in my fancy, there's no great harm done. If he's nothing more than a marionette, let him fall on the floor, and stay there until I find some imaginative writer who will take him off my hands - you, for instance. You can have Bonetti for a Christmas present, with my compliments. I'm through with him; but as for Miss Andrews, she has been so confoundedly elusive that she has aroused my deepest interest, and I couldn't give her up if I wanted to. I never encountered a heroine like her in all my life before, and the one object of my future career will be to catch her finally in the meshes of a romance. Romance will come into her life some time. She is not at all of an unsentimental nature - only fractious - new-womanish, perhaps; but none the less lovable, and Cupid will have a shot at her when she least expects it; and when it does come, I'll be on hand to report the attempted assassination for the delectation of the Herring, Beemer, & Chadwick public."

"I should think you would try a little persuasion, just for larks," I suggested.

"You forget I am a realist," he replied, as he went out.

Now I sincerely admired Stuart Harley, and I wished to the bottom of my heart to help him if I could. It seemed to me that, however admirable Miss Andrews had shown herself to be generally as a woman, she had been an altogether unsatisfactory person in the role of a heroine. I respected her scruples about marrying men she did not care for, and, as I have already said, no one could deny her the right to her own convictions; but it seemed to me that in the Bonetti incident she might and truly ought to have acted differently when the time came for the presentation. There is no doubt in my mind that her little speech to Willard, in which she stated that the

Count was a fraud and might not be presented, was a deliberately planned rebuff, and therefore not in any sense excusable. She could have avoided it by telling Willard before leaving home that she did not care to meet the Count. To make a scene at Mrs. Howlett's was not a thing which a sober-minded, self-contained woman would have done; it was bad form to behave so rudely to one of Mrs. Howlett's guests, and was so inconsiderate of Willard and unreasonable in other ways that I blamed her unreservedly.

"She deserves to be punished," I thought to myself, as Harley went dejectedly out of the room. "And there is no kind of punishment for a woman like that so galling to her soul as to find herself in the hands of a relentless despot who forces her this way and that, according to his whim. I'd like to play Petrucio to her Katherine for five minutes. She'd soon find out that I'm not a realist bound by a creed to which I must adhere. Whatever I choose to do I can do without violating my conscientious scruples, because I haven't any conscientious scruples in literature. And, by Jove, I'll do it! I'll take Miss Marguerite Andrews in hand myself this very afternoon, and I'll put her through a course of training that will make her rue the day she ever trifled with Stuart Harley - and when he takes her up again she'll be as meek as Moses."

Strong in my belief that I could bring the young woman to terms, I went to my desk and tried my hand at a story, with Miss Andrews as its heroine, and I was not particular about being realistic either. Neither did I go off into any trances in search of heroes and villains. I did what Harley could not do. I brought the New York back to port that very day, and despatched Robert Osborne, the despised lover of the first tale, to Newport.

"She shall have him whether she likes him or not," said I, gritting my teeth determinedly; "and she won't know whether she loves him or Count Bonetti best; and she'll promise to marry both of them; and she shall go to Venice in August, despite her uncompromising refusal to do so for Harley; and she shall meet Balderstone there, and, no matter what her opinion of him or of his literary work, she shall be fascinated by the story I'll have him write, and under the spell of that fascination she shall promise to marry him also; whereupon the Willards will turn up and take her to Heidelberg, where I'll have her meet the hero she couldn't wait for at the Howlett dance, the despised Professor, and she shall promise to be his wife likewise; and finally I'll put her on board a steamer at Southampton, bound for New York, with Mrs. Corwin and the twins; and the second day out, when she is feeling her very worst, all four of her fiances will turn up at the same time beside her chair. Then I shall leave her to get out of her trouble the best way she can. I imagine, after she has had a taste of my literary regimen, she'll quite fall in love with the Harley method, and behave herself as a heroine should."

I sat down all aglow with the idea of being able to tame Harley's heroine and place her in a mood more suited for his purposes. The more I thought of how his failures were weighing on his mind, the more viciously ready was I to play the tyrant with Marguerite, and - well, I might as well confess it at once, with all my righteous indignation against her, I could not do it. Five times I started, and as many times did I destroy what I wrote. On the sixth trial I did haul the New York relentlessly back into port, never for an instant considering the inconvenience of the passengers, or the protests of the officers, crew, or postal authorities. This done, I seized upon the unfortunate Osborne, spirited his luggage through the

Custom-house, and sent the ship to sea again. That part was easy. I have written a great deal for the comic papers, and acrobatic nonsense of that sort comes almost without an effort on my part. With equal ease I got Osborne to Newport - how, I do not recollect. It is just possible that I took him through from New York without a train, by the mere say-so of my pen. At any rate, I got him there, and I fully intended to have him meet Miss Andrews at a dance at the Ocean House the day after his arrival. I even progressed so far as to get up the dance. I described the room, the decorations, and the band. I had Osborne dressed and waiting, with Bonetti also dressed and waiting on the other side of the room, Scylla and Charybdis all over again, but by no possibility could I force Miss Andrews to appear. Why it was, I do not pretend to be able to say - she may have known that Bonetti was there, she may have realized that I was trying to force Osborne upon her; but whatever it was that enabled her to do so, she resisted me successfully - or my pen did; for that situation upon which I had based the opening scene of my story of compulsion I found beyond my ability to depict; and as Harley had done before me, so was I now forced to do - to change my plan.

"I'll have her run away with!" I cried, growing vicious in my wrath; "and both Bonetti and Osborne shall place her under eternal obligations by rushing out to stop the horse, one from either side of the street. She'll have to meet Bonetti then," I added, with a chuckle.

And I tried that plan. As docile as a lamb she entered the phaeton, which I conjured up out of my ink-pot, and like a veteran Jehu did she seize the reins. I could not help admiring her as I wrote of it - she was so like a goddess; but I did not relent. Run away with she must be, and run away with she was. But again did this extraordinary woman assert herself to my discomfiture; for the moment she saw Bonetti rushing out to rescue her from the east, she jerked the left rein so violently that the horse swerved to one side, toppled over on Osborne, who had sprung gallantly to the rescue from the west; and Bonetti, missing his aim as the horse turned, fell all in a heap in the roadway two yards back of the phaeton. Miss Andrews was not hurt, but my story was, for she had not even observed the unhappy Osborne; and as for Bonetti, he cut so ridiculous a figure that, Italian though he was, even he seemed aware of it, and he shrank dejectedly out of sight. Again had this supernaturally elusive heroine upset the plans of one who had essayed to embalm her virtues in a literary mould. I could not bring her into contact with either of my heroes.

I threw my pen down in disgust, slammed to the cover of my ink-well, and for two hours paced madly through the maze-like walks of the Central Park, angry and depressed; and from that moment until I undertook the narration of this pathetic story I gave Harley's heroine up as unavailable material for my purposes. She was worse, if anything, in imaginative work than in realism, because she absolutely defied the imagination, while the realist she would be glad to help so long as his realism was kept in strict accord with her ideas of what the real really was.

It was some days before I saw Harley again, and I thought he looked tired and anxious - so anxious, indeed, that I was afraid he might possibly be in financial straits, for I knew that for three weeks he had not turned out any of his usual pot-boilers, having been too busy trying to write the story for Messrs. Herring, Beemer, & Chadwick. It happened, oddly enough, that I had two or three uncashed checks in my pocket; so, feeling like a millionaire, I broached the subject to him.

"What's the matter, old fellow?" I said. "You seem in a blue funk. Has the mint stopped? If it has, command me. I'm overburdened with checks this week."

"Not at all; thanks just the same," he said, wearily. "My Tiffin royalties came in Wednesday, and I'm all right for a while, anyhow."

"What's up, then, Stuart?" I asked. "You look worried. I've just offered to share my prosperity with you, you might share your grief with me. Lend me a peck of trouble overnight, will you?"

"Oh, it's nothing much," he said. "It's that rebellious heroine of mine. She's weighing on my mind, that's all. She's very real to me, that woman; and, by Jove! I've been as jealous as a lover for two days over a fancy that came into my head. You'll laugh when I tell you, but I've been half afraid somebody else would take her up and - well, treat her badly. There is something that tells me that she has been forced into some brutal situation by somebody, somewhere, within the past two or three days. I believe I'd want to kill a man who did that."

I didn't laugh at him. I was the man who was in a fair way to get killed for "doing that," and I thought laughter would be a little bit misplaced; but I am not a coward, and I didn't flinch. I confessed. I tried to ease his mind by telling him what I had attempted to do.

"It was a mistake," he said, shortly, when I had finished. "And you must promise me one thing," he added, very seriously.

"I'll promise anything," I said, meekly.

"Don't ever try anything of the sort again," he went on, gravely. "If you had succeeded in writing that story, and subjected her to all that horror, I should never have spoken to you again. As it is, I realize that what you did was out of the kindness of your heart, prompted by a desire to be of service to me, and I'm just as much obliged as I can be, only I don't want any assistance."

"Until you ask me to, Stuart," I replied, "I'll never write another line about her; but you'd better keep very mum about her yourself, or get her copyrighted. The way she upset that horse on Osborne, completely obliterating him, and at the same time getting out of the way of that little simian Count, in spite of all I could do to place her under obligations to both of them, was what the ancients would have called a caution. She has made a slave of me forever, and I venture to predict that if you don't hurry up and get her into a book, somebody else will; and whoever does will make a name for himself alongside of which that of Smith will sink into oblivion."

"Count on me for that," said he. "'Faint heart never won fair lady,' and I don't intend to stop climbing just because I fear a few more falls."

CHAPTER VI

ANOTHER CHAPTER FROM HARLEY

"Was ever woman in this humour woo'd?
Was ever woman in this humour won?
I'll have her, - but I will not keep her long."

"RICHARD III."

There was no doubt about it that Harley, true to his purpose, was making a good fight to conquer without compulsion, and appreciated as much as I the necessity of reducing his heroine to concrete form as speedily as possible, lest some other should prove more successful, and so deprive him of the laurels for which he had worked so hard and suffered so much. In his favor was his disposition. He was a man of great determination, and once he set about doing something he was not an easy man to turn aside, and now that, for the first time in his life, he found himself baffled at every point, and by a heroine of no very great literary importance, he became more determined than ever.

"I'll conquer yet," he said to me, a week or so later; but the weariness with which he spoke made me fear that victory was afar off.

"I've no doubt of it - ultimately," I answered, to encourage him; "but don't you think you'll stand a better chance if you let her rest for a while, and then steal in upon her unawares, and catch her little romance as it flies? She is apparently nerved up against you now, and the more conscious she is of your efforts to put her on paper, the more she will rebel. In fact, her rebelliousness will become more and more a matter of whim than of principle, unless you let up on her for a little while. Half of her opposition now strikes me as obstinacy, and the more you try to break her spirit, even though you do it gently, the more stubborn will she become. Put this book aside for a few weeks anyhow. Why not tackle something else? You'd do better work, too, after a little variety."

"This must be finished by September 1st, that's why not," said Stuart. "I've promised Herring, Beemer, & Chadwick to send them the completed manuscript by that time. Besides, no heroine of mine shall ever say that she swerved me from doing what I have set about doing. It is now or never with Marguerite Andrews."

So I left him at his desk, and for a week was busy with my own affairs. Late the following Friday night I dropped in at Harley's rooms to see how matters were progressing. As I entered I saw him at his desk, his back turned towards me, silhouetted in the lamp-light, scratching away furiously with his pen.

"Ah!" I thought, as my eye took in the picture, "it goes at last. I guess I won't disturb his train of thought."

And I tried to steal softly out, for he had not observed my entrance. As luck would have it, I stepped upon the sill of the door as I passed out, and it creaked.

"Hello!" cried Harley, wheeling about in his chair, startled by the sound.

"Oh! It's you, is it?" he added, as he recognized me. "What are you up to? Come back here. I want to see you."

His manner was cheerful, but I could see that the cheerfulness was assumed. The color had completely left his cheeks, and great rings under his eyes betokened weariness of spirit.

"I didn't want to disturb you," said I, returning. "You seem to have your pen on a clear track, with full steam up."

"I had," he said, quietly. "I was just finishing up that Herring, Beemer, & Chadwick business."

"Aha!" I cried, grasping his hand and shaking it. "I congratulate you. Success at last, eh?"

"Well, I've got something done - and that's it," he said, and he tossed the letter block upon which he had been writing across the table to me. "Read that, and tell me what you think of it."

I read it over carefully. It was a letter to Messrs. Herring, Beemer, & Chadwick, in which Stuart asked to be relieved of the commission he had undertaken:

> "I find myself utterly unable to complete the work in the stipulated time," he wrote, "for reasons entirely beyond my control. Nor can I at this

writing say with any degree of certainty when I shall be able to finish the story. I have made constant and conscientious effort to carry out my agreement with you, but fruitlessly, and I beg that you will relieve me of the obligation into which I entered at the signing of our contract. Of course I could send you something long enough to cover the required space - words come easy enough for that - but the result would be unsatisfactory to you and injurious to me were I to do so. Please let me hear from you, releasing me from the obligation, at your earliest convenience, as I am about to leave town for a fortnight's rest. Regretting my inability to serve you at this time, and hoping soon to be able to avail myself of your very kind offer, I beg to remain,

"Yours faithfully,

"STUART HARLEY."

"Oh!" said I. "You've finished it, then, by -"

"By giving it up," said he, sadly.

"It's the strangest thing that ever happened to me, but that girl is impossible. I take up my pen intending to say that she did this, and before I know it she does that. I cannot control my story at all, nor can I perceive in what given direction she will go. If I could, I could arrange my scenario to suit, but as it is, I cannot go on. It may come later, but it won't come now, and I'm going to give her up, and go down to Barnegat to fish for ten days. I hate to give the book up, though," he added, tapping the table with his pen-holder reflectively. "Chadwick's an awfully good fellow, and his firm is one of the best in the country, liberal and all that, and here at my first opportunity to get on their list, I'm completely floored. It's beastly hard luck, I think."

"Don't be floored," said I. "Take my advice and tackle something else. Write some other book."

"That's the devil of it!" he replied, angrily pounding the table with his fist. "I can't. I've tried, and I can't. My mind is full of that woman. If I don't get rid of her I'm ruined - I'll have to get a position as a salesman somewhere, or starve, for until she is caught between good stiff board covers I can't write another line."

"Oh, you take too serious a view of it, Stuart," I ventured. "You're mad and tired now. I don't blame you, of course, but you mustn't be rash. Don't send that letter yet. Wait until you've had the week at Barnegat - you'll feel better then. You can write the book in ten days after your return; or if you still find you can't do it, it will be time enough to withdraw then."

"What hope is there after that?" he cried, tossing a bundle of manuscript into my lap. "Just read that, and tell me what's the use. I'd mapped out a meeting between Marguerite Andrews and a certain Mr. Arthur Parker, a fellow with wealth, position, brains, good looks - in short, everything a girl could ask for, and that's what came of it."

I spread the pages out upon the table before me and read:

CHAPTER VII

A DECLARATION

*"I have not seen
So likely an ambassador of love."*

"Merchant of Venice."

Parker mounted the steps lightly and rang the bell. Marguerite's kindness of the night before, which was in marked contrast to her coolness at the MacFarland dance, had led him to believe that he was not wholly without interest to her, and her invitation that he should call upon her had given him a sincere pleasure; in fact, he wondered that he should be so pleased over so trivial a circumstance.

"I'm afraid I've lost my heart again," he said to himself. "That is, again if I ever lost it before," he added.

And his mind reverted to a little episode at Bar Harbor the summer before, and he was not sorry to feel that that wound was cured - though, as a matter of fact, it had never amounted to more than a scratch.

A moment later the door opened, and Parker entered,

inquiring for Miss Andrews as he did so.

"I do not know, but I will see if Miss Andrews is at home," said the butler, ushering him into the parlor. That imposing individual knew quite well that Miss Andrews was at home, but he also knew that it was not his place to say so until the young lady had personally assured him of the facts in so far as they related to this particular caller. All went well for Parker, however. Miss Andrews consented to be at home to him, and five minutes later she entered the drawing room where Parker was seated.

"How do you do?" she said, frigidly, ignoring his outstretched hand.

("Think of that, will you?" interposed Harley. "He'd come to propose, and was to leave engaged, and she insists upon opening upon him frigidly, ignoring his outstretched hand."

I couldn't help smiling. "Why did you let her do it?" I asked.

"I could no more have changed it than I could fly," returned Stuart. "She ought never to have been at home if she was going to behave that way. I couldn't foresee the incident, and before I knew it that's the way it happened. But I thought I could fix it up later, so I went on. Read along, and see what I got let into next."

I proceeded to read as follows:)

"You see," said Parker, with an admiring glance at her eyes, in spite of the fact that the coolness of her reception rather abashed him - "you see, I have not delayed very long in coming."

"So I perceive," returned Marguerite, with a bored manner. "That's what I said to Mrs. Willard as I came down. You don't allow your friends much leeway, Mr. Parker. It doesn't seem more than five minutes since we were together at the card party."

("That's cordial, eh?" said Harley, as I read. "Nice sort of talk for a heroine to a hero. Makes it easy for me, eh?"

"I must say if you manage to get a proposal in now you're a genius," said I.

"Oh - as for that, I got reckless when I saw how things were going," returned Harley. "I lost my temper, and took it out of poor Parker. He proposes, as you will see when you come to it; but it isn't realism - it's compulsion. I simply forced him into it - poor devil. But go on and read for yourself."

I did so, as follows:)

This was hardly the treatment Parker had expected at the hands of one who had been undeniably gracious to him at the card-table the night before. He had received the notice that she was to be his partner at the tables with misgivings, on his arrival at Mrs. Stoughton's, because his recollection of her behavior towards him at the MacFarland dance had led him to believe that he was personally distasteful to her; but as the evening at cards progressed he felt instinctively drawn towards her, and her vivacity of manner, cleverness at repartee, and extreme amiability towards himself had completely won his heart, which victory their little tete-a-tete during supper had confirmed. But here, this morning, was reversion to her first attitude.

What could it mean? Why should she treat him so?

("I couldn't answer that question to save my life," said Stuart. "That is, not then, but I found out later. I put it in, however, and let Parker draw his own conclusions. I'd have helped him out if I could, but I couldn't. Go on and see for yourself."

I resumed.)

Parker could not solve the problem, but it pleased him to believe that something over which he had no control had gone wrong that morning, and that this had disturbed her equanimity, and that he was merely the victim of circumstances; and somehow or other it pleased him also to think that he could be the victim of her circumstances, so he stood his ground.

"It is a beautiful day," he began, after a pause.

"Is it?" she asked, indifferently.

("Frightfully snubbish," said I, appalled at the lengths to which Miss Andrews was going.

"Dreadfully," sighed Harley. "And so unlike her, too.")

"Yes," said Parker, "so very beautiful that it seemed a pity that you and I should stay indoors, with plenty of walks to be taken and -"

Marguerite interrupted him with a sarcastic laugh.

"With so much pity and so many walks, Mr. Parker, why

don't you take a few of them!" she said.

("Good Lord!" said I. "This is the worst act of rebellion yet. She seems beside herself."

"Read on!" said Harley, in sepulchral tones.)

This was Parker's opportunity. "I am not fond of walking, Miss Andrews," he said; and then he added, quickly, "that is, alone - I don't like anything alone. Living alone, like walking alone, is -"

"Let's go walking," said Marguerite, shortly, as she rose up from her chair. "I'll be down in two minutes. I only need to put my hat on."

Parker acquiesced, and Miss Andrews walked majestically out of the parlor and went up-stairs.

"Confound it!" muttered Parker, as she left him. "A minute more, and I'd have known my fate."

("You see," said Harley, "I'd made up my mind that that proposal should take place in that chapter, and I thought I'd worked right up to it, in spite of all Miss Andrews's disagreeable remarks when, pop - off she goes to put on her hat."

"Oh - as for that - that's all right," said I. "Parker had suggested the walk, and a girl really does like to stave off a proposal as long as she can when she knows it is sure to come. Furthermore, it gives you a chance to describe the hat, and so make up for a few of the words you lost when she refused to discuss ball-dresses with Mrs. Willard."

"I never thought of that; but don't you think I worked

up to the proposal skilfully?" asked Harley.

"Very," said I. "But you're dreadfully hard on Parker. It would have been better to have had the butler fire him out, head over heels. He could have thrashed the butler for doing that, but with your heroine his hands were tied."

"Go on and read," said Harley.)

"She must have known what I was driving at," Parker reflected, as he awaited her return. "Possibly she loves me in spite of this frigid behavior. This may be her method of concealing it; but if it is, I must confess it's a case of

'Perhaps it was right to dissemble your love,
But - why did you kick me down-stairs?'

Certainly, knowing, as she now must, what my feelings are, her being willing to go for a walk on the cliffs, or anywhere, is a favorable sign.

("Parker merely echoed my own hope in that remark," said Harley. "If I could get them engaged, I was satisfied to do it in any way that might be pleasing to her.")

A moment later Marguerite appeared, arrayed for the walk. Parker rose as she entered and picked up his gloves.

"You are a perfect picture this morning," said he.

"I'm ready," she said, shortly, ignoring the compliment. "Where are we scheduled to walk? - or are we to have something to say about it ourselves?"

Parker looked at her with a wondering smile. The aptness

of the remark did not strike him. However, he was equal to the occasion.

"You don't believe in free will, then?" he asked.

("It was the only intelligent remark he could make, under the circumstances, you see," explained Harley.

"He was a clever fellow," said I, and resumed reading.)

"I believe in a great many things we are supposed to do without," said Marguerite, sharply.

They had reached the street, and in silence walked along Bellevue Avenue.

"There are a great many things," vouchsafed Parker, as they turned out of the avenue to the cliffs, "that men are supposed not to do without -"

"Yes," said Margucrite, sharply - "vices."

"I did not refer to them," laughed Parker. "In fact, Miss Andrews, the heart of man is supposed to be incomplete until he has lost it, and has succeeded in getting another for his very -"

"Are you an admirer of Max Nordau?" interposed Marguerite, quickly.

("Whatever led you to put that in?" I asked.

"Go on, and you'll see," said Harley. "I didn't put it in. It's what she said. I'm not responsible.")

"I don't know anything about Max Nordau," said

Parker, somewhat surprised at this sudden turn of the conversation.

"Are you familiar with Schopenhauer?" she asked.

("It was awfully rough on the poor fellow," said Harley, "but I couldn't help him. I'd forced him in so far that I couldn't get him out. His answer floored me as completely as anything that Miss Andrews ever did.")

"Schopenhauer?" said Parker, nonplussed. "Oh yes," he added, an idea dawning on his mind. "That is to say, moderately familiar - though, as a matter of fact, I'm not at all musical."

Miss Andrews laughed immoderately, in which Parker, thinking that he had possibly said something witty, although he did not know what it was, joined. In a moment the laughter subsided, and for a few minutes the two walked on in silence. Finally Parker spoke, resignedly.

"Miss Andrews," he said, "perhaps you have noticed - perhaps not - that you have strongly interested me."

"Yes," she said, turning upon him desperately. "I have noticed it, and that is why I have on two separate occasions tried to keep you from saying so."

"And why should I not tell you that I love -" began Parker.

"Because it is hopeless," retorted Marguerite. "I am perfectly well aware, Mr. Parker, what we are down for, and I suppose I cannot blame you for your persistence. Perhaps you don't know any better; perhaps you do know better, but are willing to give yourself over unreservedly into the hands of another; perhaps you are being forced and cannot help yourself. It is just possible that you are a professional hero, and feel under obligations to your employer to follow out his wishes to the letter. However it may be, you have twice essayed to come to the point, and I have twice tried to turn you aside. Now it is time to speak truthfully. I admire and like you very much, but I have a will of my own, am nobody's puppet, and if Stuart Harley never writes another book in his life, he shall not marry me to a man I do not love; and, frankly, I do not love you. I do not know if you are aware of the fact, but it is true nevertheless that you are the third fiance he has tried to thrust upon me since July 3d. Like the others, if you insist upon blindly following his will, and propose marriage to me, you shall go by the board. I have warned you, and you can now do as you please. You were saying - ?"

"That I love you with all my soul," said Parker, grimly.

("He didn't really love her then, you know," said Harley. "He'd been cured of that in five minutes. But I was resolved that he should say it, and he did. That's how he came to say it grimly. He did it just as a soldier rushes up to the cannon's mouth. He added, also:")

"Will you be my wife?"

"Most certainly not," said Marguerite, turning on her heel, and leaving the young man to finish his walk alone.

("And then," said Harley, with a chuckle, "Parker's manhood would assert itself in spite of all I could do. He made an answer, which I wrote down.")

"I see," said I, "but you've scratched it out. What was that line?"

"'"Thank the Lord!" said Parker to himself, as Miss Andrews disappeared around the corner,'" said Stuart Harley. "That's what I wrote, and I flatter myself on the realism of it, for that's just what any self-respecting hero would have said under the circumstances."

A silence came over us.

"Do you wonder I've given it up," asked Stuart, after a while.

"Yes," said I, "I do. Such opposition would nerve me up to a battle royal. I wouldn't give it up until I'd returned from Barnegat, if I were you," I added, anxious to have him renew his efforts; for an idea had just flashed across my mind, which, although it involved a breach of faith on my part, I nevertheless believed to be good and justifiable, since it might relieve Stuart Harley of his embarrassment.

"Very well," I rejoiced to hear him say. "I won't give it up until then, but I haven't much hope after that last chapter."

So Harley went to Barnegat, after destroying his letter to Messrs. Herring, Beemer, & Chadwick, whilst I put my breach of faith into operation.)

CHAPTER VIII

A BREACH OF FAITH

"Having sworn too hard-a-keeping oath,
Study to break it, and not to break my troth."

"LOVE'S LABOR'S LOST."

When I assured Harley that I should keep my hands off
his heroine until he requested me to do otherwise, after
my fruitless attempt to discipline her into a less refractory
mood, I fully intended to keep my promise. She was his,
as far as she possessed any value as literary material, and
he had as clear a right to her exclusive use as if she had
been copyrighted in his name - at least so far as his
friends were concerned he had. Others might make use
of her for literary purposes with a clear conscience if they
chose to do so, but the hand of a friend must be stayed.
Furthermore, my own experience with the young woman
had not been successful enough to lead me to believe that
I could conquer where Harley had been vanquished.
Physical force I had found to be unavailing. She was too
cunning to stumble into any of the pitfalls that with all
my imagination I could conjure up to embarrass her; but

something had to be done, and I now resolved upon a course of moral suasion, and wholly for Harley's sake. The man was actually suffering because she had so persistently defied him, and his discomfiture was all the more deplorable because it meant little short of the ruin of his life and ambitions. The problem had to be solved or his career was at an end. Harley never could do two things at once. The task he had in hand always absorbed his whole being until he was able to write the word finis on the last page of his manuscript, and until the finis to this elusive book he was now struggling with was written, I knew that he would write no other. His pot-boilers he could do, of course, and so earn a living, but pot-boilers destroy rather than make reputations, and Harley was too young a man to rest upon past achievements; neither had he done such vastly superior work that his fame could withstand much diminution by the continuous production of ephemera. It was therefore in the hope of saving him that I broke faith with him and temporarily stole his heroine. I did not dream of using her at all, as you might think, as a heroine of my own, but rather as an interesting person with ideas as to the duty of heroines - a sort of Past Grand Mistress of the Art of Heroism - who was worth interviewing for the daily press. I flatter myself it was a good idea, worthy almost of a genius, though I am perfectly well aware that I am not a genius. I am merely a man of exceptional talent. I have talent enough for a genius, but no taste for the unconventional, and by just so much do I fall short of the realization of the hopes of my friends and fears of my enemies. There are stories I have in mind that are worthy of the most exalted French masters, for instance, and when I have the time to be careful, which I rarely do, I can write with the polished grace of a De Maupassant or a James, but I shall never write them, because I value my social position too highly to put my name to anything which it would never do to publish outside of Paris. I do not care to prove my genius at the cost of the respect of my neighbors - all of which, however, is foreign to my story, and is put in here merely because I have observed that readers are very much interested in their favorite authors, and like to know as much about them as they can.

My plan, to take up the thread of my narrative once more, was, briefly, to write an interview between myself, as a representative of a newspaper syndicate, and Miss Marguerite Andrews, the "Well-Known Heroine." It has been quite common of late years to interview the models of well-known artists, so that it did not require too great a stretch of the imagination to make my scheme a reasonable one. It must be remembered, too, that I had no intention of using this interview for my own aggrandizement. I planned it solely in the interests of my friend, hoping that I might secure from Miss Andrews some unguarded admission that might operate against her own principles, as Harley and I knew them, and that, that secured, I might induce her to follow meekly his schedule until he could bring his story to a reasonable conclusion. Failing in this, I was going to try and discover what style of man it was she admired most, what might be her ideas of the romance in which she would most like to figure, and all that, so that I could give Harley a few points which would enable him so to construct his romance that his heroine would walk through it as easily and as docilely as one could wish. Finally, all other things failing, I was going to throw Harley on her generosity, call attention to the fact that she was ruining him by her stubborn behavior, and ask her to submit to a little temporary inconvenience for his sake.

As I have already said, so must I repeat, there was genius in the idea, but I was forced to relinquish certain features of it, as will be seen shortly. I took up my pen, and with three bold strokes thereof transported myself to Newport, and going directly to the Willard Cottage, I rang the bell. Miss Andrews was still elusive. With all the resources of imagination at hand, and with not an obstacle in my way that I could not clear at a bound, she still held me at bay. She was not at home - had, in fact, departed two days previously for the White Mountains. Fortunately, however, the butler knew her address, and, without bothering about trains, luggage, or aught else, in one brief paragraph I landed myself at the Profile House, where she was spending a week with Mr. and Mrs. Rushton of Brooklyn. This change of location caused me to modify my first idea, to its advantage. I saw, when I thought the matter over, that, on the whole, the interview, as an interview for a newspaper syndicate, was likely to be nipped in the bud, since the moment I declared myself a reporter for a set of newspapers, and stated the object of my call, she would probably dismiss me with the statement that she was not a professional heroine, that her views were of no interest to the public, and that, not having the pleasure of my acquaintance, she must beg to be excused. I wonder I didn't think of this at the outset. I surely knew Harley's heroine well enough to have foreseen this possibility. I realized it, however, the moment I dropped myself into the great homelike office of the Profile House. Miss Andrews walked through the office to the dining-room as I registered, and as I turned to gaze upon her as she passed majestically on, it flashed across my mind that it would be far better to appear before her as a fellow-guest, and find out what I wanted and tell her why I had come in that guise, rather than introduce myself as one of those young men who earn their daily bread by poking their noses into other people's business.

Had this course been based upon any thing more solid than a pure bit of imagination, I should have found it difficult to accommodate myself so easily to circum-stances. If it had been Harley instead of myself, it would have been impossible, for Harley would never have stooped to provide himself with a trunk containing fresh linen and evening-dress clothes and patent-leather pumps by a stroke of his pen. This I did, however, and that evening, having created another guest, who knew me of old and who also was acquainted with Miss Andrews, just as I had created my excellent wardrobe, I was presented.

The evening passed pleasantly enough, and I found Harley's heroine to be all that he had told me and a great deal more besides. In fact, so greatly did I enjoy her society that I intentionally prolonged the evening to about three times its normal length - which was a very inartistic bit of exaggeration, I admit; but then I don't pretend to be a realist, and when I sit down to write I can make my evenings as long or as short as I choose. I will say, however, that, long as my evening was, I made it go through its whole length without having recourse to such copy-making subterfuges as the description of doorknobs and chairs; and except for its unholy length, it was not at all lacking in realism. Miss Andrews fascinated me and seemed to find me rather good company, and I found myself suggesting that as the next day was Sunday she take me for a walk. From what I knew of Harley's experience with her, I judged she'd be more likely to go if I asked her to take me instead of offering to take her. It was a subtle distinction, but with some women subtle distinctions are chasms which men must not try to overleap too vaingloriously, lest disaster overtake them.

My bit of subtlety worked like a charm. Miss Andrews graciously accepted my suggestion, and I retired to my couch feeling certain that during that walk to Bald Mountain, or around the Lake, or down to the Farm, or wherever else she might choose to take me, I could do much to help poor Stuart out of the predicament into which his luckless choice of Miss Andrews as his heroine had plunged him. And I wasn't far wrong, as the event transpired, although the manner in which it worked out was not exactly according to my schedule.

I dismissed the night with a few paragraphs; the morning, with its divine service in the parlor, went quickly and impressively; for it IS an impressive sight to see gathered beneath those towering cliffs a hundred or more of pleasure and health seekers of different creeds worshipping heartily and simply together, as accordantly as though they knew no differences and all men were possessed of one common religion - it was too impressive, indeed, for my pen, which has been largely given over to matters of less moment, and I did not venture to touch upon it, passing hastily over to the afternoon, when Miss Andrews appeared, ready for the stroll.

I gazed at her admiringly for a moment, and then I began:

"Is that the costume you wore" - I was going to say, "when you rejected Parker?" but I fortunately caught my error in time to pass it off - "at Newport?" I finished, with a half gasp at the narrowness of my escape; for, it must be remembered, I was supposed as yet to know nothing of that episode.

"How do you know what I wore at Newport?" she asked,

quickly - so quickly that I almost feared she had found me out, after all.

"Why - ah - I read about you somewhere," I stammered. "Some newspaper correspondent drew a picture of the scene on the promenade in the afternoon, and - ah - he had you down."

"Oh!" she replied, arching her eyebrows; "that was it, was it? And do you waste your valuable time reading the vulgar effusions of the society reporter?"

Wasn't I glad that I had not come as a man with a nose to project into the affairs of others - as a newspaper reporter!

"No, indeed," I rejoined, "not generally; but I happened to see this particular item, and read it and remembered it. After all," I added, as we came to the sylvan path that leads to the Lake - "after all, one might as well read that sort of stuff as most of the novels of the present day. The vulgar reporter may be ignorant or a boor, and all that is reprehensible in his methods, but he writes about real flesh and blood people; and, what is worse, he generally approximates the truth concerning them in his writing, which is more than can be said of the so-called realistic novel writers of the day. I haven't read a novel in three years in which it has seemed to me that the heroine, for instance, was anything more than a marionette, with no will of her own, and ready to do at any time any foolish thing the author wanted her to do."

Again those eyes of Miss Andrews rested on me in a manner which gave me considerable apprehension. Then she laughed, and I was at ease again.

"You are very amusing," she said, quietly. "The most amusing of them all."

The remark nettled me, and I quickly retorted:

"Then I have not lived in vain."

"You do really live, then, eh?" she asked, half chaffingly, gazing at me out of the corners of her eyes in a fashion which utterly disarmed me.

"Excuse me, Miss Andrews," I answered, "but I am afraid I don't understand you."

"I am afraid you don't," she said, the smile leaving her lips. "The fact that you are here on the errand you have charged yourself with proves that."

"I am not aware," I said, "that I have come on any particularly ridiculous errand. May I ask you what you mean by the expression 'most amusing of them all'? Am I one among many, and, if so, one what among many what?"

"Your errand is a good one," she said, gravely, "and not at all ridiculous; let me assure you that I appreciate that fact. Your question I will answer by asking another: Are you here of your own volition, or has Stuart Harley created you, as he did Messrs. Osborne, Parker, and the Professor? Are you my new hero, or what?"

The question irritated me. This woman was not content with interfering seriously with my friend's happiness: she was actually attributing me to him, casting doubts upon my existence, and placing me in the same category with herself - a mere book creature. To a man who regards himself as being the real thing, flesh and blood, and, well, eighteen-carat flesh and blood at that, to be accused of living only a figmentary existence is too much. I retorted angrily.

"If you consider me nothing more than an idea, you do not manifest your usual astuteness," I said.

Her reply laid me flat.

"I do not consider you anything of the sort. I never so much as associated you with anything resembling an idea. I merely asked a question," she said. "I repeat it. Do you or do you not exist? Are you a bit of the really real or a bit of Mr. Harley's realism? In short, are you here at Profile Lake, walking and talking with me, or are you not?"

A realizing sense of my true position crept over me. In reality I was not there talking to her, but in my den in New York writing about her. I may not be a realist, but I am truthful. I could not deceive her, so I replied, hesitatingly:

"Well, Miss Andrews, I am - no, I am not here, except in spirit."

"That's what I thought," she said, demurely. "And do you exist somewhere, or is this a 'situation' calculated to delight the American girl - with pin-money to spend on Messrs. Herring, Beemer, & Chadwick's publications?"

"I do exist," I replied, meekly; for, I must confess it, I realized more than ever that Miss Andrews was too much for me, and I heartily wished I was well out of it. "And I alone am responsible for this. Harley is off fishing at

Barnegat - and do you know why?"

"I presume he has gone there to recuperate," she said.

"Precisely," said I.

"After his ungentlemanly, discourteous, and wholly uncalled-for interference with my comfort at Newport," she said, her face flushing and tears coming into her eyes, "I don't wonder he's prostrated."

"I do not know to what you refer," said I.

"I refer to the episode of the runaway horse," she said, in wrathful remembrance of the incident. "Because I refuse to follow blindly his will, he abuses his power, places me in a false and perilous situation, from which I, a defenceless woman, must rescue myself alone and unaided. It was unmanly of him - and I will pay him the compliment of saying wholly unlike him."

I stood aghast. Poor Stuart was being blamed for my act. He must be set right at once, however unpleasant it might be for me.

"He - he didn't do that," I said, slowly; "it was I. I wrote that bit of nonsense; and he - well, he was mad because I did it, and said he'd like to kill any man who ill-treated you; and he made me promise never to touch upon your life again."

"May I ask why you did that?" she asked, and I was glad to note that there was no displeasure in her voice - in fact, she seemed to cheer up wonderfully when I told her that it was I, and not Stuart, who had subjected her to the misadventure.

"Because I was angry with you," I answered. "You were ruining my friend with your continued acts of rebellion: he was successful; now he is ruined. He thinks of you day and night - he wants you for his heroine; he wants to make you happy, but he wants you to be happy in your own way; and when he thinks he has discovered your way, he works along that line, and all of a sudden, by some act wholly unforeseen, and, if I may say so, unforeseeable, you treat him and his work with contempt, draw yourself out of it - and he has to begin again."

"And why have you ventured to break your word to your friend?" she asked, calmly. "Surely you are touching upon my life now, in spite of your promise."

"Because I am willing to sacrifice my word to his welfare," I retorted; "to try to make you understand how you are blocking the path of a mighty fine-minded man by your devotion to what you call your independence. He will never ask you to do anything that he knows will be revolting to you, and until he has succeeded in pleasing you to the last page of his book he will never write again. I have done this in the hope of persuading you, at the cost even of some personal discomfort, not to rebel against his gentle leadership - to fall in with his ideas until he can fulfil this task of his, whether it be realism or pure speculation on his part. If you do this, Stuart is saved. If you do not, literature will be called upon to mourn one who promises to be one of its brightest ornaments."

I stopped short. Miss Andrews was gazing pensively out over the mirror-like surface of the Lake. Finally she spoke.

"You may tell Mr. Harley," she said, with a sigh, "that I will trouble him no more. He can do with me as he pleases in all save one particular. He shall not marry me to a man I do not love. If he takes the man I love for my hero, then will I follow him to the death."

"And may I ask who that man is?"

"You may ask if you please," she replied, with a little smile. "But I won't answer you, except to say that it isn't you."

"And am I forgiven for my runaway story?" I asked.

"Yes," she said. "You wouldn't expect me to condemn a man for loyalty to his friend, would you?"

With which understanding Miss Andrews and I continued our walk, and when we parted I found that the little interview I had started to write had turned into the suggestion of a romance, which I was in duty bound to destroy - but I began to have a glimmering of an idea as to who the man was that Marguerite Andrews wished for a hero, and I regretted also to find myself convinced of the truth of her statement that that man did not bear my name.

CHAPTER IX

HARLEY RETURNS TO THE FRAY

"I will be master of what is mine own:
She is my goods, my chattels."

"TAMING OF THE SHREW."

At the end of ten days Harley returned from Barnegat, brown as a berry and ready for war, if war it was still to be. The outing had done him a world of good, and the fish stories he told as we sat at dinner showed that, realist though he might be, he had yet not failed to cultivate his imagination in certain directions. I may observe in passing, and in this connection, that if I had a son whom it was my ambition to see making his mark in the world as a writer of romance, as distinguished from the real, I should, as the first step in his development, take care that he became a fisherman. The telling of tales of the fish he caught when no one else was near to see would give him, as it has given many another, a good schooling in the realms of the imagination.

I was glad to note that Harley's wonted cheerfulness had returned, and that he had become more like himself than he had been at any time since his first failure with Miss Andrews.

"Your advice was excellent," he said, as we sipped our coffee at the club the night of his return. "I have a clear two weeks in which to tackle that story, and I feel confident now that I shall get it done. Furthermore, I shall send the chapters to Herring, Beemer, & Chadwick as I write them, so that there must be no failure. I shall be compelled to finish the tale, whatever may happen, and Miss Andrews shall go through to the bitter end, willy-nilly."

"Don't be rash, Harley," I said; for it seemed to me that Miss Andrews, having consented at my solicitation to be a docile heroine for just so long as Harley did not insist upon her marrying the man she did not love, it was no time for him to break away from the principles he had so steadfastly adhered to hitherto and become a martinet. He struck me as being more than likely to crack the whip like a ring-master in his present mood than to play the indulgent author, and I felt pretty confident that the instant the snap of the lash reached the ears of Marguerite Andrews his troubles would begin again tenfold, both in quality and in quantity, with no possible hope for a future reconciliation between them.

"I'm not going to be rash," said Harley. "I never was rash, and I'm not going to begin now, but I shall use my nerve. That has been the trouble with me in the past. I haven't been firm. I have let that girl have her own way in everything, and I'm very much afraid I have spoiled her. She behaves like a child with indulgent parents. In the last instance, the Parker proposal, she simply ran her independence into the ground. She was not only rebellious to me, but she was impertinent to him. Her attitude toward him was not nature at all; it was not realism, because she is a woman of good breeding, and would naturally be the last to treat any man, distasteful or not, with such excessive rudeness. I compelled him to go on and propose to her, though after he had been at it for five minutes I could see that he wished he was well out of it. I should have taken her in hand and controlled her with equal firmness, declining to permit her to speak so openly. Frankness is good enough, especially in women, among whom you rarely find it; but frankness of the sort she indulged in has no place in the polite circle in which she moves."

"Nevertheless, she spoke that way - you said yourself she did," I said, seeing that he was wrathful with Marguerite, and wishing to assuage his anger before it carried him to lengths he might regret. "And you've got to take her as she is or drop her altogether."

"She did - I repeat that she did speak that way, but that was no reason why I should submit to it," Harley answered. "It was the fault of her mood. She was nervous, almost hysterical - thanks to her rebellious spirit. The moment I discovered how things were going I should have gone back and started afresh, and kept on doing so until I had her submissive. A hunter may balk at a high fence, but the rider must not give in to him unless he wishes to let the animal get the better of him. If he is wise he will go back and put the horse to it again and again, until he finally clears the topmost bar. That I should have done in this instance, and that I now intend to do, until that book comes out as I want it."

I had to laugh in my sleeve. On the whole, Harley was very like most other realists, who pretend that they merely put down life as it is, and who go through their professional careers serenely unconscious of the truth that their fancies, after all, serve them when their facts are lacking. Even that most eminent disciple of the Realistic Cult, Mr. Darrow, has been known to kill off a hero in a railroad accident that owed its being to nothing short of his own imagination, in order that the unhappy wight might not offend the readers of the highly moral magazine, in which the story first appeared, by marrying a widow whom he had been forced by Mr. Darrow to love before her husband died. Mr. Darrow manufactured, with five strokes of his pen, an engine and a tunnel to crush the life out of the poor fellow, whom an immoral romancer would have allowed to live on and marry the lady, and with perfect propriety too, since the hero and the heroine were both of them the very models of virtue, in spite of the love which they did not seek, and which Mr. Darrow deliberately and almost brutally thrust into their otherwise happy lives. Of course the railway accident was needed to give the climax to the story, which without it might have run through six more numbers of the magazine, to the exclusion of more exciting material; but that will not relieve Mr. Darrow's soul of the stain he has put upon it by deserting Dame Realism for a moment to flirt with Romance, when it comes to the Judgment Day.

"As I want it to be, so must it be," quoth Harley.

"Good," thought I. "It will no doubt be excellent; but be honest, and don't insist that you've taken down life as it is; for you may have an astigmatism, for all you know, and life may not be at all what it has seemed to you while you were putting it down."

"Yes, sir," said Harley, leaning back in his chair and drawing a long breath, which showed his determination, "to the bitter end she shall go, through such complications as I choose to have her, encountering whatever villains I may happen to find most convenient, and to complete her story she shall marry the man I select for my hero, if he is as commonplace as the average salesman in a Brooklyn universal dry-goods emporium."

Imagine my feelings if you can! Having gone as a self-appointed ambassador to the enemy to secure terms of peace, to return to find my principal donning his armor and daubing his face with paint for a renewal of the combat, was certainly not pleasant. What could I say to Marguerite Andrews if I ever met her in real life? How could I look her in the eye? The situation overpowered me, and I hardly knew what to say. I couldn't beg Harley to stick to his realism and not indulge in compulsion, because I had often jeered at him for not infusing a little more of the dramatic into his stories, even if it had to be "lugged in by the ears," as he put it. Nor was he in any mood for me to tell him of my breach of faith - the mere knowledge that she had promised to be docile out of charity would have stung his pride, and I thought it would be better, for the time, at least, to let my interview remain a secret. Fortune favored me, however. Kelly and the Professor entered the dining room at this moment, and the Professor held in his hand a copy of the current issue of The Literary Man, Messrs. Herring, Beemer, & Chadwick's fortnightly publication, a periodical having to do wholly with things bookish.

"Who sat for this, Stuart?" called out the Professor, tapping the frontispiece of the magazine.

"Who sat for what?" replied Stuart, looking up.

"This picture," said the Professor.

"It's a picture of a finely intellectual-looking person with your name under it, Harley," put in the Doctor.

"Oh - that," said Harley. "It does flatter me a bit."

"So does the article with it," said Kelly. "Says you are a great man - man with an idea, and all that. Is that true, or is it just plain libel? Have you an idea?"

Harley laughed good-naturedly. "I had one once, but it's lost," he said. "As to that picture, they're bringing out a book for me," he added, modestly. "Good ad., you know."

"When you are through with that, Professor," I put in, "let me have it, will you? I want to see what it says about Harley."

"It's a first-rate screed," replied the Professor, handing over the publication. "It hits Harley right on the head."

"I don't know as that's pleasant," said Harley.

"What I mean, my dear boy," said the Professor, "is that it does you justice."

And it really did do Harley justice, although, as he had suggested, it was written largely to advertise the forth-coming work. It spoke nicely of Harley's previous efforts, and judiciously, as it seemed to me. He had not got to the top of the ladder yet, but he was getting there by a slow, steady development, and largely because he was a man with a fixed idea as to what literature ought to be.

"Mr. Harley has seen clearly from the outset what it was that he wished to accomplish and how to accomplish it," the writer observed. "He has swerved neither to the right nor to the left, but has progressed undeviatingly along the lines he has mapped out for himself, and keeping constantly in mind the principles which seemed to him at the beginning of his career to be right. It has been this persistent and consistent adherence to principle that has gained for Mr. Harley his hearing, and which is constantly rendering more certain and permanent his position in the world literary. Others may be led hither and yon by the fads and follies of the scatter-brained, but Realism will ever have one steadfast champion in Stuart Harley."

"Read that," I said, tossing the journal across the table.

He read it, and blushed to the roots of his ears.

"This is no time to desert the flag, Harley," said I, as he read. "Stick to your colors, and let her stick to hers. You'd better be careful how you force your heroine."

"Ha, ha!" he laughed. "I should think so, and for more reasons than one. I never really intended to do horrible things with her, my boy. Trust me, if I do lead her, to lead her gently. My persuasion will be suggestive rather than mandatory."

"And that hero - from the Brooklyn dry-goods shop?" I asked, with a smile.

"I'd like to see him so much as - tell her the price of anything," cried Harley. "A man like that has no business to live in the same hemisphere with a woman like Marguerite Andrews. When I threatened her with him I was conversing through a large and elegant though wholly invisible hat."

I breathed more freely. She was still sacred and safe in his hands. Shortly after, dinner over, we left the table, and went to the theatre, where we saw what the programme called the "latest London realistic success," in which three of the four acts of an intensely exciting melodrama depended upon a woman's not seeing a large navy revolver, which lay on the table directly before her eyes in the first. The play was full of blood and replete with thunder, and we truly enjoyed it, only Harley would not talk much between the acts. He was unusually moody. After the play was over his tongue loosened, however, and we went to the Players for a supper, and there he burst forth into speech.

"If Marguerite Andrews had been the heroine of that play she'd have seen that gun, and the audience would have had to go home inside of ten minutes," he said. Later on he burst out with, "If my Miss Andrews had been the heroine of that play, the man who falls over the precipice in the second act would have been alive at this moment." And finally he demanded: "Do you suppose a heroine like Marguerite Andrews would have overlooked the comma on the postal card that woman read in the third act, and so made the fourth act possible? Not she. She's a woman with a mind. And yet they call that the latest London realistic success! Realistic! These Londoners do not seem to understand their own language. If that play was realism, what sort of a nightmare do you suppose a romantic drama would be?"

"Well, maybe London women in real life haven't any minds," I said, growing rather weary of the subject. I admired Miss Andrews myself, but there were other things I could talk about - "like lemonade and elephants," as the small boy said. "Let it go at that. It was an interesting play, and that's all plays ought to be.

Realism in plays is not to be encouraged. A man goes to the theatre to be amused and entertained, not to be reminded of home discomforts."

Stuart looked at me reproachfully, ordered a fresh cigar, and suggested turning in for the night. I walked home with him and tried to get him interested in a farce I was at work on, but it was of no use. He had become a monomaniac, and his monomania was his rebellious heroine. Finally I blurted out:

"Well, for Heaven's sake, Stuart, get the woman caged, will you? For, candidly, I'd like to talk about something else, and until Marguerite Andrews is disposed of I don't believe you'll be able to."

"I'll have half the work done by this time to-morrow night," said he. "I've got ten thousand words of it in my mind now."

"I'll bet you there are only two words down in your mind," said I.

"What are they?" he asked.

"Marguerite and Andrews," said I.

Stuart laughed. "They're the only ones I'm sure of," said he. And then we parted.

But he was right about what he would have accomplished by that time the next night; for before sundown he had half the story written, and, what is more, the chapters had come as easily as any writing he ever did. For docility, Marguerite was a perfect wonder. Not only did she follow out his wishes; she often anticipated them, and in certain parts gave him a lead in a new direction, which, Stuart said, gave the story a hundred per cent. more character.

In short, Marguerite Andrews was keeping her promise to me nobly. The only thing I regretted about it, now that all seemed plain sailing, was its effect on Stuart. Her amiability was proving a great attraction to his susceptible soul, and I was beginning to fear that Stuart was slowly but surely falling in love with his rebellious heroine, which would never do, unless she were really real, on which point I was most uncertain.

"It would be a terrible thing," said I confidentially to myself, "if Stuart Harley were to fall in love with a creation of his own realism."

CHAPTER X

A SUMMONS NORTH

"PORTIA. A quarrel, ho, already? What's the matter?
"GRATIANO. About a hoop of gold, a paltry ring."

"MERCHANT OF VENICE."

The events just narrated took place on the 15th of August, and as Harley's time to fulfil his contract with Messrs. Herring, Beemer, & Chadwick was growing very short - two weeks is short shrift for an author with a book to write for waiting presses, even with a willing and helpful cast of characters - so I resolved not to intrude upon him until he himself should summon me. I knew myself, from bitter experience, how unwelcome the most welcome of one's friends can be at busy hours, having had many a beautiful sketch absolutely ruined by the untimely intrusion of those who wished me well, so I resolutely kept myself away from his den, although I was burning with curiosity to know how he was getting on.

On occasions my curiosity would get the better of my judgment, and I would endeavor, with the aid of my own muses, to hold a moment's chat with Miss Andrews;

but she eluded me. I couldn't find her at all - as, indeed, how should I, since Harley had not taken me into his confidence as to his intentions in the new story? He might have laid the scene of it in Singapore, for aught I knew, and, wander where I would in my fancy, I was utterly unable to discover her whereabouts, until one evening a very weird thing happened - a thing so weird that I have been pinching myself with great assiduity ever since in order to reassure myself of my own existence. I had come home from a hard day's editorial work, had dined alone and comfortably, and was stretched out at full length upon the low divan that stands at the end of my workshop - the delight of my weary bones and the envy of my friends, who have never been able to find anywhere another exactly like it. My cigar was between my lips, and above my head, rising in a curling cloud to the ceiling, was a mass of smoke. I am sure I was not dreaming, although how else to account for it I do not know. What happened, to put it briefly, was my sudden transportation to a little mountain hotel not far from Lake George, where I found myself sitting and talking to the woman I had so futilely sought.

"How do you do?" said she, pleasantly, as I materialized at her side.

"I am as well as a person can be," I replied, rubbing my eyes in confusion, "who suddenly finds himself two hundred and fifty miles away from the spot where, a half-hour before, he had lain down to rest."

Miss Andrews laughed. "You see how it is yourself," she said.

"See how what is myself?" I queried.

"To be the puppet of a person who - writes," she answered.

"And have I become that?" I asked.

"You have," she smiled. "That's why you are here."

The idea made me nervous, and I pinched my arm to see whether I was there or not. The result was not altogether reassuring. I never felt the pinch, and, try as I would, I couldn't make myself feel it.

"Excuse me," I said, "for deviating a moment from the matter in hand, but have you a hat-pin?"

"No," she answered; "but I have a brooch, if that will serve your purpose. What do you want it for?"

"I wish to run it into my arm for a moment," I explained.

"It won't help you any," she answered, smiling divinely. "I must have a word with you; all the hat-pins in the world shall not prevent me, now that you are here."

"Well, wait a minute, I beg of you," I implored. "You intimated a moment ago that I was a puppet in the hands of some author. Whose? I've a reputation to sustain, and shall not give myself up willingly, unless I am sure that that person will not trifle with my character."

"Exactly my position," said she. "As I said, you can now understand how it is yourself. But I will tell you in whose hands you are now - you are in mine. Surely if you had the right to send me tearing down Bellevue Avenue at

Newport behind a runaway horse, and then pursue me in spirit to the Profile House, I have the right to bring you here, and I have accordingly done so."

For a woman's, her logic was surprisingly convincing. She certainly had as much right to trifle with my comfort as I had to trifle with hers.

"You are right, Miss Andrews," I murmured, meekly. "Pray command me as you will - and deal gently with the erring."

"I will treat you far better than you treated me," she said. "So have no fear - although I have been half minded at times to revenge myself upon you for that runaway. I could make you dreadfully uncomfortable, for when I take my pen in hand my imagination in the direction of the horrible is something awful. I shall be merciful, however, for I believe in the realistic idea, and I will merely make use of the power my pen possesses over you to have you act precisely as you would if you were actually here."

"Then I am not here?" I queried.

"What do you think?' she asked, archly.

I was about to say that if I weren't, I wished most heartily that I were; but I remembered fortunately that it would never do for me to flirt with Stuart Harley's heroine, so I contented myself with saying, boldly, "I don't know what to think."

Miss Andrews looked at me for a moment, and then, reaching out her hand, took mine, pressed it, and relinquished it, saying, "You are a loyal friend indeed."

There was nothing flirtatious about the act; it was a simple and highly pleasing acknowledgment of my forbearance, and it made me somewhat more comfortable than I had been at any time since my sudden transportation through the air.

"You remember what I said to you?" she resumed. "That I would cease to rebel, whatsoever Mr. Harley asked me to do, unless he insisted upon marrying me to a man I did not love?"

"I do," I replied. "And, as far as I am aware, you have stuck by your agreement. Stuart, I doubt not, has by this time got ready for his finishing-touches."

"Your surmise is correct," she answered, sadly; and then, with some spirit, she added: "And they are finishing-touches with a vengeance. I have been loyal to my word, in spite of much discomfort. I have travelled from pillar to post as meekly as a lamb, because it fitted in with Stuart Harley's convenience that I should do so. He has taken me and my friend Mrs. Willard to and through five different summer resorts, where I have cut the figure he wished me to cut without regard to my own feelings. I have discussed all sorts of topics, of which in reality I know nothing, to lend depth to his book. I have snubbed men I really liked, and appeared to like men I profoundly hated, for his sake. I have wittingly endured peril for his sake, knowing of course that ultimately he would get me out of danger; but peril is peril just the same, and to that extent distracting to the nerves. I have been upset in a canoe at Bar Harbor, and lost on a mountain in Vermont. I have sprained my ankle at Saratoga, and fainted at a dance at Lenox; but no complaint have I uttered - not even the suggestion of a rebellion have I given. Once, I admit, I was disposed to resent his desire that I should wear a certain costume, which he, man as he is, could not see would be wofully unbecoming. Authors have no business to touch on such things. But I overcame the temptation to rebel, and to please him wore a blue and pink shirt-waist with a floral silk skirt at a garden-party - I suppose he thought floral silk was appropriate to the garden; nor did I even show my mortification to those about me. Nothing was said in the book about its being Stuart Harley's taste; it must needs be set down as mine; and while the pages of Harley's book contain no criticism of my costume, I know well enough what all the other women thought about it. Still, I stood it. I endured also without a murmur the courtship and declaration of love of a perfect booby of a man; that is to say, he was a booby in the eyes of a woman - men might like him. I presume that as Mr. Harley has chosen him to stand for the hero of his book, he must admire him; but I don't, and haven't, and sha'n't. Yet I have pretended to do so; and finally, when he proposed marriage to me I meekly answered 'yes,' weeping in the bitterness of my spirit that my promise bound me to do so; and Stuart Harley, noting those tears, calls them tears of joy!"

"You needn't have accepted him," I said, softly. "That wasn't part of the bargain."

"Yes, it was," she returned, positively; "that is, I regarded it so, and I must act according to my views of things. What I promised was to follow his wishes in all things save in marriage to a man I didn't love. Getting engaged is not getting married, and as he wished me to get engaged, so I did, expecting of course that the book would end there, as it ought to have done, and that therefore no marriage would ever come of the engagement."

"Certainly the book should end there, then," said I. "You have kept to the letter of your agreement, and nobly," I added, with enthusiasm, for I now saw what the poor girl must have suffered. "Harley didn't try to go further, did he?"

"He did," she said, her voice trembling with emotion. "He set the time and place for the wedding, issued the cards, provided me with a trousseau - a trousseau based upon his intuitions of what a trousseau ought to be, and therefore about as satisfactory to a woman of taste as that floral silk costume of the garden-party; he engaged the organist, chose my bridesmaids - girls I detested - and finally assembled the guests. The groom was there at the chancel rail; Mr. Willard, whom he had selected to give me away, was waiting outside in the lobby, clad in his frock-coat, a flower in his button-hole, and his arm ready for the bride to lean on; the minister was behind the rail; the wedding-march was sounding -"

"And you?" I cried, utterly unable to contain myself longer.

"I was speeding past Yonkers on the three-o'clock Saratoga express - bound hither," she answered, with a significant toss of her head. "No one but yourself knows where I am, and I have summoned you to explain my action before you hear of it from him. I do not wish to be misjudged. Stuart Harley had his warning, but he chose to ignore it, and he can get out of the difficulty he has brought upon himself in his own way - possibly he will destroy the whole book; but I wanted you to know that while he did not keep the faith, I did."

I suddenly realized the appalling truth. My own weakness was responsible for it all. I had not told Harley of my interview and her promise, feeling that it was not necessary, and fearing its effect upon his pride.

"I may add," she said, quietly, "that I am bitterly disappointed in your friend. I was interested in him, and believed in him. Most of my acts of rebellion - if you can call me rebellious - were prompted by my desire to keep him true to his creed; and I will tell you what I have never told to another: I regarded Stuart Harley almost as an ideal man, but this has changed it all. If he was what I thought him, he could not have acted with so little conscience as to try to force this match upon me, when he must have known that I did not love Henry Dunning."

"He didn't know," I said.

"He should have been sure before providing for the ceremony, after hearing what I had promised you I would and would not do," said Marguerite.

"But - I never told him anything about your promise!" I shouted, desperately. "He has done all this unwittingly."

"Is that true? Didn't you tell him?" she cried, eagerly grasping my hand.

Her manner left no doubt in my mind as to who the hero of her choice would be - and again I sighed to think that it was not I.

"As true as that I stand here," I said. "I never told him."

She shrugged her shoulders.

"Oh, well, you know what I mean!" I said, excitedly.

"Wherever I do stand, it's as true as that I stand there."

The phrase was awkward, but it fulfilled its purpose.

"Why didn't you tell him?" she asked.

"Because I didn't think it necessary. Fact is," I added, "I had a sort of notion that if you married anybody in one of Harley's books, if Harley had his own way it would be to the man who - who tells the sto -"

A loud noise interrupted my remark and I started up in alarm, and in an instant I found myself back in my rooms in town once more. The little mountain house near Lake George, with its interesting and beautiful guest, had faded from sight, and I realized that somebody was hammering with a stick upon my door.

"Hello there!" I cried. "What's wanted?"

"It's I - Harley," came Stuart's voice. "Let me in."

I unlocked the door and he entered. The brown of Barnegat had gone, and he was his broken self again.

"Well," I said, trying to ignore his appearance, which really shocked me, "how's the book? Got it done?"

He sank into a chair with a groan.

"Hang the book! - it's all up with that; I'm going to Chadwick to-morrow and call the thing off," he said. "She won't work - two weeks' steady application gone for nothing."

"Oh, come!" I said; "not as bad as that."

"Precisely as bad as that," he retorted. "What can a fellow do if his heroine disappears as completely as if the earth had opened and swallowed her up?"

"Gone?" I cried, with difficulty repressing my desire to laugh.

"Completely - searched high and low for her - no earthly use," he answered. "I can't even imagine where she is."

"All of which, my dear Stuart," I said, adopting a superior tone for the moment, "shows that an imagination that is worth something wouldn't be a bad possession for a realist, after all. I know where your heroine is. She is at a little mountain house near Lake George, and she has fled there to escape your booby of a hero, whom you should have known better than to force upon a girl like Marguerite Andrews. You're getting inartistic, my dear boy. Sacrifice something to the American girl, but don't sacrifice your art. Just because the aforesaid girl likes her stories to end up with a wedding is no reason why you should try to condemn your heroine to life-long misery."

Stuart looked at me with a puzzled expression for a full minute.

"How the deuce do you know anything about it?" he asked.

I immediately enlightened him. I told him every circumstance - even my suspicion as to the hero of her heart, and it seemed to please him.

"Won't the story go if you stop it with the engagement?" I asked, after it was all over.

"Yes," he said, thoughtfully. "But I shall not publish it. If it was all so distasteful to her as you say, I'd rather destroy it."

"Don't do that," I said. "Change the heroine's name, and nobody but ourselves will ever be the wiser."

"I never thought of that," said he.

"That's because you've no imagination," I retorted.

Stuart smiled. "It's a good idea, and I'll do it; it won't be the truest realism, but I think I am entitled to the leeway on one lapse," he said.

"You are," I rejoined. "Lapse for the sake of realism. The man who never lapses is not real. There never was such a man. You might change that garden-party costume too. If you can't think of a better combination than that, leave it to me. I'll write to my sister and ask her to design a decent dress for that occasion."

"Thanks," said Stuart, with a laugh. "I accept your offer; but, I say, what was the name of the little mountain house where you found her?"

"I don't know," I replied. "You made such an infernal row battering down my door that I came away in a hurry and forgot to ask."

"That is unfortunate," said Stuart. "I should have liked to go up there for a while - she might help me correct the proofs, you know."

That's what he said, but he didn't deceive me. He loved her, and I began again to hope to gracious that Harley had not deceived himself and me, and that Marguerite Andrews was a bit of real life, and not a work of the imagination.

At any rate, Harley had an abiding faith in her existence, for the following Monday night he packed his case and set out for Lake George. He was going to explore, he said.

CHAPTER XI

BY WAY OF EPILOGUE

"Let, down the curtain, the farce is done."

RABELAIS.

I suppose my story ought to end here, since Harley's rebellious heroine has finally been subdued for the use of his publishers and the consequent declaration of dividends for the Harley exchequer; but there was an epilogue to the little farce, which nearly turned it into tragedy, from which the principals were saved by nothing short of my own ingenuity. Harley had fallen desperately in love with Marguerite Andrews, and Marguerite Andrews had fallen in love with Stuart Harley, and Harley couldn't find her. She eluded his every effort, and he began to doubt that he had drawn her from real life, after all. She had become a Marjorie Daw to him, and the notion that he must go through life cherishing a hopeless passion was distracting to him. His book was the greatest of his successes, which was an additional cause of discomfort to him, since, knowing as he now did that his study was not a faithful portrayal of the inner life of his heroine, he felt that the laurels that were being placed upon his brow had been obtained under false pretences.

"I feel like a hypocrite," he said, as he read an enthusiastic review of his little work from the pen of no less a person than Mr. Darrow, the high-priest of the realistic sect. "I am afraid I shall not be able to look Darrow in the eye when I meet him at the club."

"Never fear for that, Stuart," I said, laughing inwardly at his plight. "Brazen it out; keep a stiff upper lip, and Darrow will never know. He has insight, of course, but he can't see as far in as you and he think."

"It's a devilish situation," he cried, impatiently striding up and down the room, "that a man of my age should be so hopelessly in love with a woman he can't find; and that he can't find her is such a cruel sarcasm upon his literary creed! What cursed idiosyncrasy of fate is it that has brought this thing upon me?"

"It's the punishment that fits your crime, Harley," I said. "You've been rather narrow minded in your literary ideas. Possibly it will make a more tolerant critic of you hereafter, when you come to flay fellows like Balderstone for venturing to think differently from you as to the sort of books it is proper to write. He has as much right to the profits he can derive from his fancy as you have to the emoluments of your insight."

"I'd take some comfort if I thought that she really loved me," he said, mournfully.

"Have no doubt on that score, Stuart," I said. "She does love you. I know that. I wish she didn't."

"Then why can't I find her? Why does she hide from me?" he cried, fortunately ignoring my devoutly expressed wish, which slipped out before I knew it.

"Because she is a woman," I replied. "Hasn't your analytical mind told you yet that the more a woman loves a man, the harder he's got to work to find it out and - and clinch the bargain?"

"I suppose you are right," he said, gloomily. "But if I were a woman, and knew I was killing a man by keeping myself in hiding, I'd come out and show myself at any cost, especially if I loved him."

"Now you are dealing in imagination, Harley," I said; "and that never was your strong point."

Nevertheless, he was right on one point. The hope-lessness of his quest was killing Harley - not physically exactly, but emotionally, as it were. It was taking all the heart out of him, and his present state of mind was far more deplorable than when he was struggling with the book, and constantly growing worse. He tried every device to find her - the Willards were conjured up, and knew nothing; Mrs. Corwin and the twins were brought back from Europe, and refused to yield up the secret; all the powers of a realistic pen were brought to bear upon her, and yet she refused utterly to materialize.

Finally, I found it necessary to act myself. I could not stand the sight of Harley being gradually eaten up by the longing of his own soul, and I tried my hand at exploration. I had no better success for several weeks; and then, like an inspiration, the whole thing came to me. "She won't come when he summons her, because she loves him. She won't summon him to come to her, for the same reason. Why not summon both of them yourself to a common ground? Embalm them in a little romance of your own. Force them if need be, but get them there, and so bring them together, and let them work out their own happiness," said I to myself. The only difficulty that presented itself was as to whether or not Marguerite would allow herself to be forced. It was worth the trial, however, and fortune favored me. I found her far from rebellious. My pen had hardly touched paper when she materialized, more bewilderingly beautiful than ever. I laid the scene of my little essay at Lake-wood, and I found her sitting down by the water, dreamily gazing out over the lake. In her lap was Stuart Harley's book, and daintily pasted on the fly-leaf of this was the portrait which had appeared in the August issue of The Literary Man, which she had cut out and preserved.

Having provided the heroine with a spot conducive to her comfort, I hastened to transport Harley to the scene. It was easy to do, seeing how deeply interested I was in my plot and how willing he was. I got him there looking like a Greek god, only a trifle more interesting, because of his sympathy-arousing pallor - the pallor which comes from an undeserved buffeting at the hands of a mischievous Cupid. I know it well, for I have observed it several times upon my own countenance. The moment Harley appeared upon the scene I chose to have Marguerite hastily clasp the book in her hands, raise it to her lips, and kiss the picture - and it must have been intensely true to life, for she did it without a moment's hesitation, almost anticipating my convenience, throwing an amount of passion into the act which made my pen fairly hiss as I dipped it into the ink. Of course Harley could not fail to see it - I had taken care to arrange all that - and equally of course he could not fail to comprehend what that kiss meant; could not fail to stop short, with a convulsive effort to control himself - heroes always do that; could not fail thereby to attract her attention. After this nothing was more natural than that she should spring to her feet, "the blushes of a surprised love mantling her cheeks"; it was equally natural that she should try to run, should slip, have him catch her arm and save her from falling, and - well, I am not going to tell the whole story. I have neither the time, the inclination, nor the talent to lay bare to the world the love-affairs of my friend. Furthermore, having got them together, I discreetly withdrew, so that even if I were to try to write up the rest of the courtship, it would merely result in my telling you how I imagined it progressed, and I fancy my readers are as well up in matters of that sort as I am. Suffice it to say, therefore, that in this way I brought Stuart Harley and Marguerite Andrews together, and that the event justified the means: and that the other day, when Mr. and Mrs. Harley returned from their honeymoon, they told me they thought I ought to give up humor and takc to writing love-stories.

"That kissing the picture episode," said Stuart, looking gratefully at me, "was an inspiration. To my mind, it was the most satisfactory thing you've ever done."

"I like that!" cried his wife, with a mischievous twinkle in her eye. "He didn't do it. It was I who kissed the picture. He couldn't have made me do anything else to save his life."

"Rebellious to the last!" said I, with a sigh to think that I must now write the word "Finis" to my little farce.

"Yes," she answered. "Rebellious to the last. I shall never consent to be the heroine of a book again, until - "

She paused and looked at Stuart.

"Until what?" he asked, tenderly.

"Until you write your autobiography," said she. "I have always wanted of be the heroine of that."

And throwing down my pen, I discovered I was alone.

Choose from Thousands of 1stWorldLibrary Classics By

Adolphus William Ward
Aesop
Agatha Christie
Alexander Aaronsohn
Alexander Kielland
Alexandre Dumas
Alfred Gatty
Alfred Ollivant
Alice Duer Miller
Alice Turner Curtis
Alice Dunbar
Ambrose Bierce
Amelia E. Barr
Andrew Lang
Andrew McFarland Davis
Anna Sewell
Annie Besant
Annie Hamilton Donnell
Annie Payson Call
Anton Chekhov
Arnold Bennett
Arthur Conan Doyle
Arthur Ransome
Atticus
B. M. Bower
Basil King
Bayard Taylor
Ben Macomber
Booth Tarkington
Bram Stoker
C. Collodi
C. E. Orr
C. M. Ingleby
Carolyn Wells
Catherine Parr Traill
Charles A. Eastman
Charles Dickens
Charles Dudley Warner
Charles Farrar Browne
Charles Ives
Charles Kingsley
Charles Lathrop Pack
Charles Whibley
Charles Willing Beale
Charlotte M. Braeme
Charlotte M.Yonge
Clair W. Hayes
Clarence Day Jr.
Clarence E. Mulford

Clemence Housman
Confucius
Cornelis DeWitt Wilcox
Cyril Burleigh
D. H. Lawrence
Daniel Defoe
David Garnett
Don Carlos Janes
Donald Keyhole
Dorothy Kilner
Dougan Clark
E. Nesbit
E.P.Roe
E. Phillips Oppenheim
Edgar Allan Poe
Edgar Rice Burroughs
Edith Wharton
Edward J. O'Biren
John Cournos
Edwin L. Arnold
Eleanor Atkins
Elizabeth Cleghorn
Gaskell
Elizabeth Von Arnim
Ellem Key
Emily Dickinson
Erasmus W. Jones
Ernie Howard Pie
Ethel Turner
Ethel Watts Mumford
Eugenie Foa
Eugene Wood
Evelyn Everett-Green
Everard Cotes
F. J. Cross
Federick Austin Ogg
Ferdinand Ossendowski
Francis Bacon
Francis Darwin
Frances Hodgson Burnett
Frank Gee Patchin
Frank Harris
Frank Jewett Mather
Frank L. Packard
Frederick Trevor Hill
Frederick Winslow Taylor
Friedrich Kerst
Friedrich Nietzsche
Fyodor Dostoyevsky

Gabrielle E. Jackson
Garrett P. Serviss
Gaston Leroux
George Ade
Geroge Bernard Shaw
George Ebers
George Eliot
George MacDonald
George Orwell
George Tucker
George W. Cable
George Wharton James
Gertrude Atherton
Grace E. King
Grant Allen
Guillermo A. Sherwell
Gulielma Zollinger
Gustav Flaubert
H. A. Cody
H. B. Irving
H. G. Wells
H. H. Munro
H. Irving Hancock
H. Rider Haggard
H. W. C. Davis
Hamilton Wright Mabie
Hans Christian Andersen
Harold Avery
Harold McGrath
Harriet Beecher Stowe
Harry Houidini
Helent Hunt Jackson
Helen Nicolay
Hendy David Thoreau
Henrik Ibsen
Henry Adams
Henry Ford
Henry Frost
Henry James
Henry Jones Ford
Henry Seton Merriman
Henry Wadsworth
Longfellow
Henry W Longfellow
Herbert A. Giles
Herbert N. Casson
Herman Hesse
Homer
Honore De Balzac

Horace Walpole
Horatio Alger, Jr.
Howard Pyle
Howard R. Garis
Hugh Lofting
Hugh Walpole
Humphry Ward
Ian Maclaren
Israel Abrahams
J.G.Austin
J. Henri Fabre
J. M. Barrie
J. Macdonald Oxley
J. S. Knowles
J. Storer Clouston
Jack London
Jacob Abbott
James Allen
James Lane Allen
James Andrews
James Baldwin
James DeMille
James Joyce
James Oliver Curwood
James Oppenheim
James Otis
Jane Austen
Jens Peter Jacobsen
Jerome K. Jerome
John Burroughs
John F. Kennedy
John Gay
John Glasworthy
John Habberton
John Joy Bell
John Milton
John Philip Sousa
Jonathan Swift
Joseph Carey
Joseph Conrad
Joseph Jacobs
Julian Hawthrone
Julies Vernes
Justin Huntly McCarthy
Kakuzo Okakura
Kenneth Grahame
Kate Langley Bosher
L. A. Abbot
L. T. Meade
L. Frank Baum
Laura Lee Hope

Laurence Housman
Leo Tolstoy
Leonid Andreyev
Lewis Carroll
Lilian Bell
Lloyd Osbourne
Louis Tracy
Louisa May Alcott
Lucy Fitch Perkins
Lucy Maud Montgomery
Lydia Miller Middleton
Lyndon Orr
M. H. Adams
Margaret E. Sangster
Margaret Vandercook
Maria Edgeworth
Maria Thompson Daviess
Mariano Azuela
Marion Polk Angellotti
Mark Overton
Mark Twain
Mary Austin
Mary Cole
Mary Rowlandson
Mary Wollstonecraft
Shelley
Max Beerbohm
Myra Kelly
Nathaniel Hawthrone
O. F. Walton
Oscar Wilde
Owen Johnson
P.G.Wodehouse
Paul and Mable Thorn
Paul G. Tomlinson
Paul Severing
Peter B. Kyne
Plato
R. Derby Holmes
R. L. Stevenson
Rabindranath Tagore
Rahul Alvares
Ralph Waldo Emmerson
Rene Descartes
Rex E. Beach
Richard Harding Davis
Richard Jefferies
Robert Barr
Robert Frost
Robert Gordon Anderson
Robert L. Drake

Robert Lansing
Robert Michael Ballantyne
Robert W. Chambers
Rosa Nouchette Carey
Ross Kay
Rudyard Kipling
Samuel B. Allison
Samuel Hopkins Adams
Sarah Bernhardt
Selma Lagerlof
Sherwood Anderson
Sigmund Freud
Standish O'Grady
Stanley Weyman
Stella Benson
Stephen Crane
Stewart Edward White
Stijn Streuvels
Swami Abhedananda
Swami Parmananda
T. S. Ackland
The Princess Der Ling
Thomas A. Janvier
Thomas A Kempis
Thomas Anderton
Thomas Bailey Aldrich
Thomas Bulfinch
Thomas De Quincey
Thomas H. Huxley
Thomas Hardy
Thomas More
Thornton W. Burgess
U. S. Grant
Valentine Williams
Victor Appleton
Virginia Woolf
Walter Scott
Washington Irving
Wilbur Lawton
Wilkie Collins
Willa Cather
Willard F. Baker
William Makepeace
Thackeray
William W. Walter
Winston Churchill
Yei Theodora Ozaki
Young E. Allison
Zane Grey